*Unfortunate
Ursula
Underwood*

Susannah B. Lewis

If you love those who love you, what credit is that to you? Even sinners love those who love them. And if you do good to those who are good to you, what credit is that to you? Even sinners do that. And if you lend to those from whom you expect repayment, what credit is that to you? Even sinners lend to sinners, expecting to be repaid in full. But love your enemies, do good to them, and lend to them without expecting to get anything back. Then your reward will be great, and you will be children of the Most High, because he is kind to the ungrateful and wicked. Be merciful, just as your Father is merciful.

Luke 6: 32-36

ONE

It was unchanging that the homeless man on the corner of 9th and Gwinnett was wearing a navy blue polyester suit, cream shirt with dingy collar and scuffed brown shoes with the rubber soles detached from the base. His dark hair was greasy but combed neatly. His mustache of brown and gray strands was well-groomed. He rested his slumped shoulders against the derelict building that once served as Starling's Hardware, and his dirty, wrinkled hands held a weathered cardboard sign with black marker faded: HUNGRY. PLEASE HELP. A chipped coffee mug of change sat next to the tattered shoes. The maroon cup read: LIVE SIMPLY. And it appeared that he did.

The homeless man never spoke when I dropped a few coins into the ceramic mug. He only shifted his blue eyes up to me for half a second, nodded and weakly smiled.

The cats of 8th Street, one gray and one orange but both thin and riddled with fleas, sat on the cracked stoop of old lady Purvis' bake shop and waited patiently for a piece of stale bread or an expired quiche. All day they scratched and they waited.

I had never favored cats. They were sneaky and quiet little devils that cared more for the food in the hand than the person attached to the hand. Yet, at that moment, as I crossed the corner of 8th and Persephone with my wool coat pulled tightly closed to shield me from the northern wind, there was a gray and white feline named Garfunkel undoubtedly perched on my living room windowsill in Downforge Alley— waiting on me, or my hand rather, to return and feed him.

Garfunkel appeared on our back porch as a kitten ten or so years before. My mother had compassion for the starved animal and declared, "One bowl of milk, then you must be on your way!" But Garfunkel had found his way, and he was not going anywhere.

The diner at 77 7th Street managed to remain among the foreclosed businesses and boarded-up shops that dominated downtown. It was a long and off-white building nestled between two vacant and broken brick structures that had once served as a flower shop and cobbler. A faded and worn burgundy awning hung over the large condensation-stained windows that lined the front of the restaurant. A blinking sign above the double swinging doors no longer illuminated, but it did not matter. There were no newcomers, out-of-towners or tourists on the south side of the Winnow River looking for a place to dine.

The air conditioner inside constantly roared no matter the season— unquestionably to keep the diner's only waitress, Bronwyn, cool. Each time patrons entered, they expected the blast of icy air to rush them.

I scuffled across the dingy black and white checkerboard floor of the quiet restaurant to my familiar table next to the payphone in the far left corner. The seat of the red booth was torn and taped, and as usual, my wool coat snagged one of the protrusions of cracked vinyl.

Galvan and Chester occupied their familiar spot near the front door— both of them pressing steaming coffee cups to their bushy, disheveled beards. Galvan chain smoked cigarettes as Chester coughed and peered out the foggy window to the abandoned steel mill across the street.

The mill had been both men's trade until it closed ten or so years before and moved its production across the sea. Hundreds were left without jobs. As the hub of downtown, the mill kept all of the businesses in the area thriving. The steelworkers piled into the hardware store on their breaks to purchase tools for projects at home. They dropped their Sunday suits at the cleaning shop on the corner of 6th and Persephone. The automotive mechanic stayed busy repairing the big trucks that hauled the steel, and the diner was bustling at lunchtime with hungry workers covered in black grime and soot. The secretaries and wives browsed the clothing shops and bought freshly baked bread from Ms. Purvis to take home for supper. The mill was the heartbeat of the south side with its fire and smoke leaving the downtown sky hazy and gray at all times.

Chester stared at the vast and vacant brick structure overshadowing the diner as bats flew in and out of the broken window panes. He was no doubt thinking of days gone by and how his life changed dramatically when that old mill's heart stopped beating. For so many years now he'd searched for reliable work but only seemed to acquire odd jobs around town. He barely made enough to feed six hungry mouths at home.

Chester's wife, Tulsee, was forced to watch other children for measly pay and often times had upwards of 15 of them in their shack on the Winnow River. Tulsee was the breadwinner, and it evidently did not set well with Chester. He spent many hours away from his home crowded with little ones, walking around town with Galvan, asking for work, painting church stoops, repairing shingles and replacing old women's light bulbs for change.

Bronwyn came out of the diner kitchen and took a drag from her cigarette resting in the bronze ashtray on the aluminum counter. She caught sight of me and gave a small wave before freshening Hamill Cooper's coffee as he sat at the shining counter and dozed in and out of consciousness after a long day of drinking bourbon. Bronwyn tapped Hamill on the shoulder to wake him and then turned and called, "Ursula's here!" to Tabb Zaxby, the diner's only cook.

"Coming right up!" I heard the large dark-skinned man

reply over the sizzling sound of the deep fryer in the kitchen.

I fidgeted with the glass salt and pepper shakers and then pulled my coat tightly around my neck to protect it from the frigid air conditioning roaring over me. Bronwyn walked toward my table with a cup of blackcurrant tea.

Bronwyn was a large woman in her late fifties who sweat profusely and often used the stained white apron covering her plain black dress to wipe perspiration from her brow. Her hair was a yellow/orange hue piled on top of her head with teased strands framing her plump face. She wore bright rouge and heavy pastel eye shadow below dark penciled-in brows. She reapplied plum lipstick after every cigarette.

"Hello, Ursula." She sat the cup of tea on the wobbly cream table.

"Bronwyn." I pulled a stirring straw from its paper coat and stuck it in the cup. "Having a good night?"

"Jemison and his crew have not been in this evening, so I cannot complain. Tabb will have your food out in," she paused and checked the thin black wristwatch squeezing her chubby wrist, "seven minutes."

The payphone beside the booth rang.

"That'll be right in time," I said.

My mother rang the payphone at the 77 7th Street Diner at precisely 7PM every Sunday.

"Hello, dear."

"Ma."

"Good things this week?" Her voice was soft and gentle as I'd always known it to be.

"I took the licorice root to Finley on Wednesday. His ulcer seems loads better for it," I paused to reminisce on the week. "On

Thursday night, Alabaster was wandering around disoriented again. I helped him get home to old man McKinley. He'd been worried sick about Alabaster. He called the squad, but they were no help."

"Very good, dear," Ma responded as I sipped the fruity tea. "Poor Mr. McKinley certainly concerns himself with Alabaster. I'm sure he was quite relieved."

"Let's see," I said, "I finished mending the quilt for the Liddell children and gave Ms. Verbena enough money to cover a week's worth of tablets. And I left my old sage coat on Penney's front stoop. I waited around to make sure she got it, but I sat across the street at the mill's loading dock so she wouldn't see me. I know she'd never accept it if she knew it were mine. She's too proud to take anything, you know. But she seemed right glad to find it after she made the long walk home from the quarry."

"I am sure she was very grateful," Ma replied. "And Oden Barmouth?"

I sighed and shook my head. "I just can't, Ma."

"But you still follow him?"

"You know I do."

"Then you know what he needs. You've seen firsthand how he is struggling."

"I cannot help but think he deserves the struggle. We certainly struggled at his hand, didn't we?"

"You must not think that way, Ursula. Oh how I pray that you will find forgiveness in your heart."

"I will always loathe Oden Barmouth. That's wrong, innit? But it's true. I possess no mercy for him."

"Does your sister know you trail him?"

"Lolly knows few of my affairs," I replied.

"She's still under Thad's spell?"

"Well of course she is, Ma! Nothing has changed since you and I last spoke. It will never change. Thad will forever be the thorn in her side."

"You aren't certain things will remain the same."

"Yes," I said, unconvinced.

"Well, on to happier things then. I have a new good thing for you to pursue. Pype Tyburn is a young man down at the soup kitchen at Mabyn Square."

"What does he require? Money? Medicine? Licorice root? I can only get so much licorice root."

"He serves at Mabyn daily. You cannot miss him. He's around your age— tall and thin with shaggy hair. You'll discover what he needs."

"Oh? He's at the soup kitchen helping others then? What can I possibly do for him? Or will he lead me to someone who needs my assistance?"

"Talk to him, Ursula. You will know," she said. "Have you any other news?"

"I sold my fourth caricature at the North Side Boardwalk last night. It was of a young girl holding a balloon. Her family was visiting from Wheatsand. They're here for the Ghost Orchid Festival. She seemed so lively, that little girl. Oh, Ma, she was so airy and bright and quite fun to draw!"

"You're talented, Ursula, but you know that," Ma spoke kindly.

"Talented? I am hardly painting chapel ceilings."

"Artistic talent is not solely found in chapels."

"I had the dream again, too, Ma. You hover over me with your finger pointed and rigidly declare that I'm to blame. I'm the one who sent you—"

"I've repeated time and time again that there's no accuracy

to that dream, Ursula. I would never blame you for my departure. You always speak as if my leaving was a punishment to you...and to me. It is not a penalty, dear. You must−"

"You keep saying it's not my burden to bear, Ma, but is it the truth?"

"Here the truth is all I know to tell, Ursula."

"I suppose." I shrugged and chewed on the end of the thin straw. "And Papa?"

"You know I can't," Ma stated adamantly.

"Is he there?" I pleaded.

"You ask every week. You know I cannot say."

"And I will continue to ask." I sighed.

"Go do good things, dear. I love you. Always."

"Always."

As I hung up the payphone, Bronwyn set my supper on the scratched table.

"Right in time." I gathered my heavy coat at my waist and slid into the ragged booth.

"Every Sunday. 7:07. Pulled pork and apple grilled cheese with crisps and blackcurrant tea. Table 7. Ursula Underwood," Bronwyn announced and walked away.

I never took the direct route home from the diner on Sunday evenings. Instead, I stirred up the rats in Dugald Alley. They scurried across my boots to the overflowing dumpster where Mr. Kestral had discarded the week's rotten vegetables and herbs. He often attempted to grow produce in his window box planter overlooking the backstreet, but he possessed a black thumb. Nothing he planted thrived. The rodents squealed and clawed at the mounds of maggot-covered tomatoes and slimy basil dropped into the dumpster from Kestral's window above.

From the alley I took a right and walked along the rusted train tracks overtaken by weeds. Cars hauling steel and coal continuously roared along that path and shook the window panes in our front room when I was a little girl. Lolly frightened at the booming sound of the quaking glass most of her young life. She was incredibly pleased Thad purchased them a home on Valoria Bend near East Dellerby Woods because it was far from the railroad.

As I walked those tracks in the winter, when the night air was crisp and cold, I could hear the faint dry rattling of the termites infesting the decayed railroad ties. After a warm rain in the summer months, the winged wood-eaters often swarmed along the railway.

Where the trees of Hannelore Park cleared, the Winnow River came into view. On the opposite bank– across the Nairn Bridge– the bright lights of the North Side Boardwalk illuminated on the calm and dark water. I could hear the distant but lively sounds of the Ghost Orchid Festival– ragtime music, passengers on the carnival rides screeching and laughing with excitement. I could see the occasional flashbulb of a camera capturing someone's cheery memory on the boardwalk.

Even when the festival wasn't taking place, the north side of the river was a very different place from my home in southern downtown. People thrived there– they really *lived* there. Even the sun shone more often on the northern ridge.

Fifty years ago, the Cronin Civil War began. It was a lengthy, tumultuous and bloody battle between the northern and southern sides of the Winnow River. The south desired equal control of the northern palladium mine, but we lost the vicious fight. Riding high on victory, North Side's Mayor Dunbryll issued a decree that all southerners and their offspring were to stay out of northern territory forever. We were allowed to keep the steel mill for a while, but now even it was gone thanks to a deal made by northern officials to have production moved across the Welshlynn Sea.

Although we were forbidden to reside there permanently, southern citizens were permitted to make short trips to the north three times per month and were required to sign the registry in northern Algirdis Square upon arrival. If anyone was caught penning a false name in the registry in hopes to acquire more visits for shopping or work per month, there were dire consequences. No one dared pencil in an alias since Tybee Watkins was publicly executed for that very thing.

Journeying to the north side was much-needed because that's where we southerners obtained our medication, clean drinking water and other supplies— including most of our food (the north side often pillaged our crops). We were also allowed to earn a small wage while there. But venturing across the Nairn Bridge was particularly dangerous. Northerners often beat and abused southerners for no valid cause other than the great prejudice that resided in their hearts. Businesses also had the right to refuse us service at any time that they wished, and officials could freely take any currency that we earned while we were there.

Although on hard times, our south side did have several pleasant areas. The blocks surrounding Mayor Kinneman's A-frame house on Gaius Hill, including Downforge Alley where I lived, weren't so bad. My mother had taken in alterations and done housework for the southern mayor all of my life, and I grew up in a small but lovely yellow house at the base of Kinneman's backyard. The train rattling our front window's glass was really the only inconvenience we had.

The Hannelore Park stretch along the murky banks of the Winnow River had always been the lowliest area downtown. Since the mill's demise, Hannelore Park had declined even more. The residents along the water were poor and desperate. Homes were often burgled, illegal medications and spirits were consumed in the abandoned shacks, and even pies weren't safe cooling in windowsills. That area along the river, all the way down to Mabyn Square, was where most of the good things were needed.

Oden Barmouth's rundown place was merely a flat-roofed wooden shed with a door and single window on the front. I knew without doubt when Oden was home because his gas lamp would be lit and he was clearly visible— a small, scrawny, greasy man sitting at a little table in the center of the lone dirt-floored room. Sometimes steam would rise from a single hole in his roof, and the smell of smoked fish would fill the crisp air, tempting other hungry rogues to take it.

Across from Oden's home was an abandoned tin shanty with a cinderblock porch. From it I had a clear view of Oden in his home— sometimes eating but most times warming his hands by the gas light and staring blankly into space. It was apparent what good things Oden needed— a heater, perhaps, and money for food other than a piece of grimy and possibly contaminated fish from the Winnow River.

Oden had continually searched for work since his release from jail a few seasons ago. Jobs were scarce for everyone on the south side but especially convicted criminals. I sometimes saw him collecting trash on the sidewalks and taking it to the sanitation department for a small reward. Other times he shined shoes for the schoolteachers who lived on Gaius Hill. Still, he didn't make enough for a decent meal. On the way to the diner one Sunday evening a few months ago, I watched him snip a piece of hard bread from the orange fleabag sitting on Ms. Purvis' 8th Street stoop.

Ma said Oden Barmouth didn't deserve to live this way despite what he'd done to our family. She longed for me to help him, but I could not bring myself to do so. I knew I saddened Ma in my thinking and deeds, or lack thereof, and I knew she continually prayed for my heart to soften toward Oden, but I did not foresee that happening.

I usually sat there and watched him for a few minutes or until I became afraid of the swarthy deplorables who shuffled along the river with ill-intent and pocket knives drawn. I wasn't sure why I sat there and watched Oden Barmouth. I did not want to help him. I knew I was putting myself in harm's way venturing to his side of town so late at night, but I found myself there every Sunday evening curiously watching the man who killed my father.

TWO

My top-floor apartment in Downforge Alley overlooked West Dellerby Woods– the very woods that separated both the northern and southern sides of the Winnow River from the vast Wheatsand Region. At the age of seven, I went to Wheatsand to see my grandmother, Ursula– my namesake.

Grandmother was a large woman– much larger than Bronwyn at the 7th Street Diner. She had fire-red curls that grazed her hips, and she wore silk dresses that draped the floor. She was very wealthy, as was all of my mother's family. In fact, everyone in Wheatsand was well-to-do.

On Ma's 16th birthday, she left Wheatsand to shop on the north side. My father, the son of a mill-worker who had always lived south of the river, had been commissioned to travel north and paint Ramsey Chapel. That's where my parents met– across the Nairn Bridge on the wealthy northern side one warm, humid evening.

My mother said it was love at first sight, but southerners like my papa weren't allowed to live in the north, and they certainly weren't allowed in Wheatsand! However, anyone could move south of the Winnow if they so desired, which no one ever did– except my mother.

Ma gave up her rights as a Wheatsand citizen, forfeited any relationship with her family and moved to the south with my papa, and she said she never regretted the decision. As she mended Mayor Kinneman's slacks and scrubbed his pot, I have to think she pondered what it would have been like if she'd stayed in Wheatsand, but she always insisted that the thought never crossed her mind.

It was very risky to sneak through West Dellerby Woods to Wheatsand, but we did just that when I was a schoolgirl. Mother dressed Lolly and me in drab brown clothes so that we'd be camouflaged in the dense forest, and we hid in the shade of the massive Runyon trees when the border patrol tram roared through the forest.

The trip through the wooded terrain took nearly two hours, but we finally emerged on the rim overlooking the far-spread region. Brannock Castle was the epicenter of Wheatsand, and my grandmother's mansion rested in its afternoon shadow. As Lolly and I stood on the ridge and took it all in, Ma pulled brightly-colored dresses that she'd sewn from her pack. Colorful apparel was the norm in Wheatsand, and we traded our brown sackcloth for paisley prints that blended us in with the ladies who strolled down the streets in radiantly-colored dresses.

Once we carefully and covertly descended to the city, mother brazenly asked the guards dressed in starched white uniforms and stationed in front of Grandmother Ursula's home to let us in. After they left us on the columned porch to confer inside for a few moments, we were eventually permitted to enter the large iron door of the manor.

Grandmother Ursula, dressed in turquoise silk, arrived in the elegant library at the front of the house to find the daughter she hadn't seen in ten years, but the reception was far from warm. She didn't acknowledge her two granddaughters in tow but immediately condemned my mother for leaving Wheatsand to live with a southern painter.

"Wheatsand is an ally of North Side, Geraldine! You've always known that. You've always known not to mingle with anyone south of the Winnow! Your father died in the Cronin Civil War when you were a child, Geraldine. A dirty southerner shot him right between the eyes as he led his troops across the Nairn

Bridge! You abandoned your family, and you abandoned your heritage in Wheatsand for a man who is probably a relative of that cold-blooded killer who took your father's life! I do not understand you, Geraldine. How did you even make it through Dellerby Woods without being shot on sight? Why are you here?" Grandmother ranted and smoked from a mahogany pipe.

"He's dead, Mother. My husband, Levon, has been dead for quite some time now." Ma wiped her damp eyes.

I'll never forget the way my large, towering Grandmother looked down on her widowed daughter— the way she looked down on all of us and callously responded, "The only good southerner is a dead one."

Ma grabbed our tiny hands and whisked us out of the mansion in the afternoon shadow of Brannock Castle. We climbed up the ridge to the woods, changed back into our colorless clothes and scurried through the forest to our home at the bottom of Gaius Hill. We never spoke of it again.

Ma never revealed the reason she riskily trekked us through the woods to visit our grandmother. I suppose she coveted comfort and wanted to introduce her mother to me— her namesake. I'm unsure. But I do know that I abhorred my name after that journey.

When I gazed out the window to West Dellerby Woods as Garfunkel purred in the sill and begged for a bite, I was always reminded of that excursion 25 years ago. I pondered if my grandmother was still alive and if I ever passed unknown aunts and uncles and cousins on my trips to North Side Boardwalk to draw caricatures. I wondered if I would ever live in a world where it wasn't forbidden to cross those woods and live in the shadow of Brannock Castle.

After imagining such folly, I retreated to my desk in the corner of the living room. The bureau that I'd purchased from Skett's Pawn when I moved to Downforge Alley was large and bulky pine. It was covered in nicks, scratches and cat hair. A soft-glowing oval lamp loomed over the typewriter and the towering stack of papers setting beside it.

Every Monday morning I retrieved the documents from Leo Magnus' office on Pascass Street. Magnus' firm was responsible for the northern palladium mine's data entry, and it was my occupation to type all of the accounting figures into forms. That type of tedious work was often contracted to southerners as our wage was cheap and the task was beneath any prominent northerner.

The stack of scribbled figures was nearly three feet high, but I managed to type every number and decimal by dark on Friday evening. After returning the pile to Leo's office and leaving the inputted information with his secretary, Mrs. Inchcape, I retrieved my paycheck and was free of the monotonous work until the following week.

By noon on Monday, my shoulders already ached from being slumped over the typewriter all morning. My eyes dazed in and out of focus and my stomach growled. I stood from the desk, stretched and walked to my small kitchenette where I ate a piece of rye bread and tossed a bite down to Garfunkel.

I pulled down my black wool coat from the hall tree and examined my face in the mirror. My long, chocolate-colored hair, the same shade as my eyes, hung loosely around my pale face and draped over my sore shoulders. Ma always said the brown hue paired well with my milky skin tone. "You are a walking glass of chocolate milk, dear daughter."

I slipped my socked feet into the black rain boots by the door, slid the dark leather gloves over my thin hands and tightened the sash of my coat. As I opened the door, I looked back to see Garfunkel leap onto the windowsill to wait on my return and another sliver of bread or possibly a chunk of salmon.

Gwinnett Avenue was a straight shot to Mabyn Square— and it was a much safer route than travelling along the waterfront. I passed the homeless man on the corner of 9th still holding the faded sign and watching the ceramic mug. I dug into the deep pocket of my coat and pulled out three coins along with a stray string from the lining. I dropped the change into the cup. As always, he never spoke. He only nodded and softly smiled.

At the corner of Gwinnett and 4th, Prentice Fawkes' wife, Staley, hung clean clothes along the line on her wooden front porch while a fat baby clung to her hip. The child's warm blue hat hung low and covered one of his eyes as he sucked on his chubby fingers and dug his round legs into his mother's small frame. I kept my head down and hoped Staley wouldn't notice me as I passed, but when I glanced over to her, she was glaring at me.

"Hello, Staley," I mumbled quietly and nodded at her, never stopping.

"Ursula," Staley smirked.

Staley's husband, Prentice, was the only boy I'd ever loved. Throughout my school days, I pathetically pined over him. For a short stint in our upper years, Prentice finally showed me some attention. He walked me home from school several times, and we even met at the diner for a weekend lunch. To say I was ecstatic would be an understatement.

However, things went sour when Staley heard that we had been courting. She made a terrible stink about it, and Prentice never spoke to me again. He'd used me to get her attention, and it had worked.

"You did not have to stoop so low as to be seen with Ursula Underwood, Prentice! That did not make me jealous. It just made me pity you! It made me want to rescue you!" Staley had exclaimed in the lunch hall before the entire student body. Although she screeched those words 15 years ago, they forever remained fresh in my memory.

I was certain that Staley reveled in the fact that she'd won Prentice Fawkes and that I was merely a drab spinster who lived with a gray and white cat. It was considered a personal triumph for her when we passed one another on the street while she donned a wedding band and a miniature Prentice on her hip.

All of the apartments along Front Street had been burned to the ground. Years ago a drunkard named Bally Treetorn had fallen asleep in his flat with a cigar in hand. The fire spread along the entire block, destroying every home and killing four— including Bally. That happened before the mill closed, and all of Bally's steel co-workers descended on the piles of ash and sang old hymns and affectionately renamed Front Street, "Bally's Way". Although the accident happened so long ago, that stretch of cobblestone was still referred to as Bally's Way and piles of charred brick would forever line the street.

Across from Bally's Way was Mabyn Square. It had once been a lovely place to convene for outdoor concerts, plays, festivals and celebrations. A statue of the city's founder, Dessick Mabyn, stood tall and proud at the center. Dessick had discovered the palladium mine and established both the northern and the southern banks of the Winnow River over 200 years ago. I often wondered what he would think of the divide between the two sides now– how we were two separate entities.

After the Cronin Civil War, northerners wanted to relocate the massive, heavy statue of Mabyn to their territory, but it proved impossible. Instead, they constructed their own statue– much grander and adorned with platinum. It greeted everyone in Algirdis Square.

Mabyn Square was littered with trash, and the homeless sheltered themselves beneath benches and lean-tos. The most coveted spot for the destitute was the base of the statue between Dessick Mabyn's concrete legs. The sculpture served as an excellent umbrella.

A tarpaulin was tied to the Runyon tree on the east side of the square and stretched to one of the columns of the former coliseum. Small fires blazed beneath the tent as the displaced huddled around them to stay warm.

A back section of the ramshackle and vandalized coliseum served as the soup kitchen. I stumbled in the dark over piles of parchment and rubble until light finally poured through a missing section of the roof. There I saw the tall, thin man with shaggy hair. It must've been Pype Tyburn.

I remained standoffish and leaned against one of the tarnished columns inside the building as I observed Pype dipping a metal ladle into a tall pot setting on a narrow table. He poured a generous helping into each bowl and topped it with crackers. He greeted every person in the line with a smile and conversation and heartily laughed on several occasions.

After watching him for a few minutes, the line finally dwindled and the homeless migrated back to the square to rest beneath the tarp or the concrete benches and slurp their warm soup. A short-statured man conversed with Pype while he wiped down the table and stirred the soup. Bracing the sharp and gusting wind, I walked into his view.

"Good afternoon, milady," he said as he grinned and reached for a cardboard bowl. "Today's specialty is minestrone made with fresh herbs and vegetables from the north side."

"Oh," I replied. "No, thank you. I'm not here to eat."

Pype looked at me confused as the icy wind blew his dark and shaggy hair across his brown eyes.

"I'm just here to observe," I clarified.

"Observe what, may I ask?"

"What you do here. I heard a man named Pype Tyburn was doing good things here, and I wanted to come and see for myself."

His face softened as he replaced the ladle into the large pot.

"I don't do these things for recognition. I just want to help."

"But good things can't help but be recognized, can they?" I asked.

"I suppose."

"Especially when it's so rare to find a good thing here," I added and looked around the dilapidated coliseum.

"You know my name. What's yours?" He handed a cleaning rag to the short, quiet man beside him and came around the table toward me.

"Ursula Underwood." I pulled the coat close to my thin body and tightened the sash.

"I've never seen you here before. I assume you live on the west side near Gaius Hill?" He tucked his hands into his clean gray apron.

"Yes. Downforge Alley," I answered. "It's rare I come this far east, although my sister does live at the edge of East Dellerby Woods on Valoria."

"Valoria is right around the corner." He nodded to his left. "Are you on your way there now?"

"No." I shook my head. "I merely came to see what good things you are doing here. And it seems," I said and looked at the line of hungry homeless forming again, "you're doing lots of good."

"I do what I can."

"How long have you been here?"

"Are you a reporter from the north side?" he questioned. "Are you here to shut me down? I purchase every ingredient legally on my allotted trips across the river. I always document what I've bought in the registry."

"Oh, no," I corrected him. "I live in Downforge Alley as I said. I just heard at the diner last night that there was a young man helping the homeless here in Mabyn Square. It's become my purpose to do good things for others, and I delight in finding others with the same goal. I enjoy seeing it firsthand."

Pype eyed me curiously for a moment before he said, "I've been down here serving for a year or so."

"Are you a permanent resident of the south? You appear to be around my age, but I do not believe we attended school together, did we?"

"No." He shook his head. "I'm a northerner by birth. I haven't been here long."

"You came here by choice or were banished?" My eyes grew wide.

"Ms. Underwood, it was my understanding that you came down here to see what good things I am doing, not to learn my life story."

I grinned. "Yes, Mr. Tyburn."

"If you'll excuse me, I must help Mr. Gunnar. He gets a bit

~ 25 ~

overwhelmed when he has to ladle *and* divvy out the crackers. Good day." He nodded at me and turned to rejoin the frazzled man behind the narrow table.

I stood there for a moment to observe Pype Tyburn serving the homeless– serving his purpose and doing his good thing. It made me smile.

THREE

I'd intended to gather the licorice root much earlier in the day, but I had been overwhelmed by the palladium mine's data entry since dawn. Racing the sunset, I hurried to dig up each root I could find in the dusky shadow of the hills. Licorice certainly wasn't native in Mabyn State, and it was a mystery how it grew in abundance during certain seasons in the deep valley at the edge of West Dellerby Woods.

Securing several roots in my khaki pack, I hiked out of the valley. The wind seemed colder and sharper than it had in weeks. I glanced at the ominous gray sky and suspected snowfall was imminent. I was thankful I'd acquired plenty of firewood from Boland Heeling's stockpile last week.

I emerged from the woods, my rubber boots soaked with mud and my wool coat covered in beggar's lice. Stubborn and clingy little devils they were. I was rarely so inattentive that I walked into a Heckalia patch, but with racing the dim light of the setting sun, it was bound to happen.

I reached Finley Skett's red wooden house on Gwinnett just as the sun vanished from the winter sky. Before I entered, I removed the muddy boots from my feet and rapped on his front door three distinctive times to signal that it was me. Finley was known to be anxious, and he was also known to keep a revolver on his lap as he wheeled around his home. I certainly didn't want to die at the hand of Skittish Skett.

Finley's home always smelled of the cinnamon and nutmeg that made up the delicious herbal tea that he consumed daily. He drank troughs of the spicy liquid which convinced me that it was partly responsible for his peptic ulcer.

"Hello, Ursula." Finley wheeled into the kitchen with the bulky, black gun on his lap. "Have you any cabbage or just licorice this visit?"

"I haven't been over the bridge to the market since last week. No cabbage. Just the licorice." I overtook his kitchen as if it were my own, turned on the tap and put murky water on the stove to boil the root.

"Very well, but you will let me pay you for it this time," he insisted.

"It grows wild, Finley. I would never charge you for anything that grows wild." I pulled the root from the khaki bag.

"But you purchase the cabbage from the northern grocer and refuse to let me repay you for it as well! You make me feel helpless, Ursula." He wheeled his chair out of the kitchen.

"That isn't my intention," I called to him.

When the licorice was on to boil, I joined Finley in his sitting room and rested on the corduroy sofa parallel to the front window. He sat across from me and read quietly by the light of a brass floor lamp. The gun was on the coffee table.

"What have you got there?" I outstretched my arms and relaxed on the worn couch.

"*Down in Carlisle* by Terrapin Greenlaw. Have you read it?" His eyes never left the book.

"Years ago," I answered. "It was quite good if I recall."

"Quite good indeed! This is my 28th read of it!"

"My mercy, Finley! Haven't you anything else to occupy your time? What about all those other books on your shelves?" I pointed to the packed bookcase.

"Oh, I read other books between. I just always come back to this one!" He held up the book with the yellow, tattered pages.

I studied Finley Skett reading in his wheelchair. He was

lanky with thinning red hair, a freckled complexion and crystal blue eyes beneath round silver-rimmed glasses. His legs were thin, shriveled and concealed by a thick brown blanket.

Finley hadn't always been crippled. When he was a young boy, he'd fallen from the Runyon tree in Mabyn Square after climbing up to get a better view of the great Gordo Riverdale playing the steel guitar during a concert.

I still remember seeing Finley fall to the cobblestone below. I was only a few yards away when he descended from the sky, and the music came to an abrupt halt. My mother pulled me close to her chest and shielded my eyes so that I would not see Finley's legs twisted like noodles.

Poor Finley's mother, Mrs. Adelaide, rushed to her little red-headed boy and cradled him in her arms as blood trickled from his forehead. In Finley's kind voice, he spoke, "I'm so sorry! I won't climb anymore Runyon trees, Mother!"

Finley was the first person I knew destined to a wheelchair, and all of the children at school gawked at him in awe. To survive such a high fall to the cobblestone was a feat in itself, but to be assigned to a woven chair with massive steel wheels only added to his popularity. We'd push him along the path in the schoolyard, and he'd laugh and spin circles around the oddly-pruned shrubs on Art Lisbon's lawn.

Before peptic ulcers plagued him so terribly, Finley often wheeled to the diner to meet me for a Thursday night meal, or we went over the Nairn Bridge together to buy groceries and browse the shops. I realized while watching him read *Down in Carlisle* for the 28th time that he truly was the best friend I'd ever known.

"How is Mrs. Adelaide getting along? And Mr. Farkas?" I interrupted the silence.

"Mother has officially lost sight in her left eye, and Pa is still having fits. Thankfully Physician Tryce is permitted one more visit to the north this month and hopes to get the remedy Pa requires."

"I hope he will, Finley," I said and stood to check on the boiling licorice.

"And your sister? Any word from Lolly?" Finley called from the sitting room.

"No word in several weeks," I replied as I poked at the soft, boiling root with a wooden spoon. "I assume she and Thad are quarreling on Valoria Bend."

"You should see her, Ursula." He wheeled his chair to the bulky kitchen table.

"Possibly."

"Certainly," he said.

"Things with Lolly are difficult, Finley. You're aware of that. Thaddeus is the thorn in her side, but she seems to endure and actually relish in the pain he inflicts upon her. I can do nothing to change her mind concerning him."

"I do understand, Ursula, but it's your duty to save your sister from his malice, innit? You must continue trying to pry them apart."

"Lolly has been a stubborn, free spirit since she was a young girl, and she's been in love with Thaddeus for nearly as long. There's nothing I can possibly do to pry them apart." I pulled the soggy root from the boiling pot and placed it in an amber-colored glass next to the stove. "How are you for money?"

"Ursula, it is not your obligation to tend to me. I appreciate the concoctions for my ulcer, but you simply cannot continue to support me monetarily."

"How are you for money?" I repeated.

"I am faring well," he lied as I handed the glass of steaming juice to him.

"Finley, I know you have been unable to work due to your ulcer. How many weeks have you been without pay now?"

"Five." Finley shifted his eyes to his small legs and looked ashamed. "Due to my absence, Pa has asked my brother to overtake the pawn shop."

I reached into the pocket of my wool coat hanging over the back of one of the dark-stained kitchen chairs and placed a bill on the table.

"You cannot do this, Ursula." He looked at the money and shook his head.

"I can. And I will."

"How can you afford this? You cannot possibly make enough at data entry to support me and yourself."

"I've done well selling caricatures this month. The Orchid Festival has proved profitable for me."

"When I'm well, Ursula," he said, "I'm going to repay you."

"You'll do no such thing, Finley Skett."

I was unsure if Pype Tyburn worked the soup kitchen at supper time, but since Finley's home was halfway to Mabyn Square, I decided to walk there and see.

As I had predicted, small snowflakes fell from the dark sky and dusted the empty streets. I wrapped my pastel pink scarf tightly around my neck, draped my long hair over my numb ears and stuffed my gloved hands deep into my wool pockets. I was not fond of the cold season. Ma had insisted it was because I had thin blood. I bled for an unusually long time even at the most minor injury. Blood poured out of me like water, Ma said. My blood failed to keep me warm.

I had never seen as many fires in Mabyn Square as I did that night. The shadows of the flames danced against the vandalized coliseum and dozens of people crowded around them, warming their hands and slurping their soup. Those not lucky enough to obtain a fireside seat huddled beneath layers of faded newsprint and shivered in the winter wind.

I reached the back of the coliseum and saw Mr. Gunnar serving beside a dark man wearing a tall white hat. The line for soup was short, but a familiar face was illuminated by the gas lanterns on the narrow table.

It was the homeless man from the corner of 9th and Gwinnett. He retrieved his paper bowl of steaming broth and shuffled right past me, the loose soles of his shoes flapping against the trash and parchment scattered on the ground.

"Sir," I called to him.

He ignored me and kept walking. The cardboard sign that he held daily was tucked beneath his bony arm, and the ceramic mug of change jingled from the pocket of his navy polyester coat.

"Sir, you oughtn't to let anyone hear the sound of your coins. You'll be robbed." I followed him but he paid me no mind. "Sir, I pass you on the corner of 9th and Gwinnett often. My name is Ursula Underwood. What's yours?"

Still he said nothing and continued to walk through the square, his shoe soles flapping and his change clinking, the steam of his soup rising into the icy night air.

I stopped while he continued and eventually disappeared into the dark shadows on Bally's Way, the faint scent of his soup remaining. I didn't know why I hadn't helped him further than merely tossing coins into his mug every few days. Doing good things for struggling southerners was my purpose, but I had neglected a man who I passed frequently. My mother so often led me to those in need of assistance, but she'd never mentioned him. I would ask her why she hadn't suggested I give new shoes to the homeless man on the corner of 9th and Gwinnett. I would ask her when we talked at the diner at 7 on Sunday evening.

From Mabyn Square, I cut through the thick row of pines to the stretch along the Winnow River where Oden Barmouth lived. His home was dark so I kept walking, curious as to why he wasn't sitting at his table warming his hands and staring at nothing.

The familiar rats in Dugald Alley dashed along the dark ground to feast on Kestral's latest failed gardening attempt. The smell of decaying, slimy kale carried on the snowflakes falling from the black sky. I pulled my scarf over my nose and marched quickly to escape the odor.

When I emerged from the alley, a woman dashed out of a flat on 3rd and scampered up the street. She seemed to be limping and from the dim streetlamp, I noticed that her coat was torn and hanging halfway off her bare shoulders.

"Ma'am?" I called to her, but she ignored me and turned right on Pascass.

I sprinted until I turned the corner and saw her resting against the teal wooden door of Leo Magnus' firm. She was out of breath, and the sound of her loud panting sliced through the cold air.

"Ma'am, is everything quite alright?" I approached her.

"Leave me be." She waved me away.

"Are you alright, ma'am?" I repeated.

"You aren't deaf, Ursula! Leave me be!"

"You know me?" I paused and slowly leaned down to examine the woman's face. "My word! Mora? Mora Sloane?"

She didn't answer. She just continued to breathe deeply and

then wiped her nose with the back of her scratched hand.

"What do you need, Mora?"

Mora straightened her back and abruptly stepped toward me. Then she demanded, "I need you to leave me be, Unfortunate Ursula Underwood!"

Only inches from my face, the scent of strong ale rolled off her breath and engulfed me. I could clearly see blood trickling from the corner of her mouth and the black bruising around her eye. Her blonde hair was ratted above her ears, and her coat was torn. It was evident she'd nearly been beaten to a pulp.

"Let me—" I reached for her arm before she angrily turned from me and limped up Pascass Street.

"I said leave me be, Unfortunate Ursula Underwood!"

I stood silently in front of my employer's office as the flakes continued to fall. In disbelief that I'd come face-to-face with Mora Sloane after so many years, I tightened the scarf around my neck once again, took a left on 4th Street and headed home.

On the frigid walk back to Downforge Alley, Mora consumed my thoughts. We were the same age, but I had not seen her in over a decade. It was rumored that she had somehow snuck over to the north side to live among the palladium brokers. Her father, old Ames Sloane, sat on his front porch on Gaius Hill every night after her disappearance and waited on his only child to return to him.

Mora Sloane found great joy in my misery. I remembered her piercing laugh when Staley ridiculed me in the lunch hall. I remembered her relentless teasing in the school yard during the elementary years as well. "Poor, pitiable Ursula! She has no daddy and her mama scrubs toilets and her sister is crazy! Prentice Fawkes will never love her, either! Ha! Ha! That pitiable thing!

Let's throw mud on her! Get her good! Unfortunate Ursula Underwood! Unfortunate Ursula Underwood! Unfortunate Ursula Underwood!"

Ma addressed the issue with Mora's parents several times over the years, but they insisted that I was a perjurer. "What blasphemous lies! Our beautiful, tender-hearted Mora would never mock a classmate."

But one day Mora Sloane disappeared. What a mystery it was on the south side! Conspiracy theories were uttered in the diner and the hardware store and the alleys. Beautiful 17-year-old Mora Sloane with her blonde locks and emerald eyes had vanished! What had become of that striking girl who would surely marry a west side businessman and live happily in a brick home on Gaius Hill?

Mr. Ames spent his allotted visits across the Nairn Bridge searching for his daughter and relentlessly checking for her name in the northern registry. When he could not find her, rumors spread that she hadn't smuggled away to the north side at all. Instead, it was supposed that she had become involved with dangerous dealings and illegal medications on the banks of the Winnow near Hannelore Park.

Old Mr. Ames was very distraught as the accusations spread and tarnished his family's reputation. He was seen searching downtown every day, and he begged the squad to be on the lookout for his daughter. When she still didn't surface, he finally declared that he'd received a letter from Mora. He wouldn't divulge any details, but he insisted that she was happy and living far from the south side. She'd managed to successfully escape, he said, and we should all be thrilled for her!

Finley argued Ames' story. He was convinced Mr. Sloane had fabricated the tale about Mora's effective escape because his daughter was, indeed, caught up with illegal medications and the ill repute of downtown. Mr. Ames lied because he simply didn't want anyone to be privy to the truth. Finley swore he'd seen Mora sticking a syringe in her arm near the Winnow one night. However, he claimed that he'd witnessed this while he was stone drunk and on his way home from Dooley Lyon's holiday party.

I'd always trusted Finley, but it was difficult to believe his story about Mora. Finley was known to exaggerate things the handful of times he had consumed anything stronger than spice tea, and Mora had been his nemesis in school, as well, so his tale about her living among the destitute was undoubtedly wishful thinking on his part. Aside from that, if Mora Sloane had remained south of the Winnow, I surely would have spotted her at some point over the years.

None of the rumors or gossip mattered now, however, because she was certainly on the south side. I'd seen her with my own eyes. And judging by her state that night on Pascass, she was the unfortunate one.

FOUR

When Papa died, Ma insisted on keeping his prized belongings, including his gold monogrammed pocket watch, straw hat and his favorite work boots covered with splatters of paint. He'd been buried in the cemetery surrounded by Runyon trees at the end of 5th Street wearing his gray Sunday suit and loafers, although he'd always joked that he wanted to be buried in his reliable boots. Ma said she just couldn't put them in the ground, though. She couldn't bear not seeing his shoes at the back door where he left them unlaced every evening after work. That's where she kept them long after he died.

Before I headed to the diner on Sunday evening, I retrieved the boots from my bedroom wardrobe. Although old and worn, they were still in reasonably good shape. They were long and heavy and the soles were completely intact. Hues of cream and blue covered the top of the boots along with a small streak of red over the left toe. I'd always questioned if the splash of crimson was paint or blood.

When I arrived at the corner of 9th and Gwinnett, the homeless man was not sitting in his usual space in front of Starling's Hardware. Instead there stood a woman digging through her purse with two small children arguing at her knees. "I can't seem to find my key," she continued to mumble.

I had not seen the homeless man from the corner since he was shuffling through Mabyn Square with a bowl of steaming broth, and I'd been very troubled about it. There were dire possibilities regarding his trek back to 9th and Gwinnett from the square. A thug possibly heard the echo of the coins clattering in his pocket and robbed and killed him in an alley. The shoes in my hand wouldn't matter to him if that were true.

When I walked into the diner on 7th Street, Jemison Alcee and his entourage were lined from one end of the aluminum counter to the other. They roared with laughter and spouted crude language as they shoveled eggs into their mouths and slammed their mugs of ale down and demanded that Bronwyn refill them.

I sat at my familiar booth in the corner, placed the shoes beside me and watched the patrons. Galvan distinguished his cigarette in a pile of half-eaten mashed sweet potatoes on his plate, grabbed his dusty hat and stood from his table. A depressed-looking Chester followed him. They exited the diner and left the noise of Jemison and his group behind.

Elsie Kipper and her adult son, Rig, also stood from their booth in the far right corner. Elsie had a look of disgust on her face as Jemison loudly told a tale riddled with obscenities. Her innocent and religious ears were certainly about to pour blood at the rhetoric.

Kind-hearted Rig Kipper patted Hamill Cooper on the back as he and his mother passed him asleep with his head on the table at the front of the restaurant. Hamill didn't startle or waken. He continued his bourbon-induced sleep, despite Jemison's gaudy conversation echoing throughout the diner.

Jemison Alcee was a gambler who lived in a red brick two-story on Gaius Hill. He was looked down on by all of his neighbors who lived in the shadow of Mayor Kinneman's home. He did not belong there.

But one night several years ago, a drunken northerner ventured downtown in an attempt to lift money off of pathetic southerners who weren't as versed in poker as he. Little did he know, Jemison Alcee was a clever card player, and the inebriated northerner lost most of his life savings to Jemison in a tense game at Lytton's Ale House on 5th Street.

The northerner attempted to leave Jemison without paying, but after a wrench's blow to the kneecap, he paid up and shamefully limped back over the Nairn Bridge.

Jemison used his winnings to purchase the home on Gaius Hill and opened it to his band of thugs. Even the squad couldn't contain the noise and ruckus coming from the house all hours of the night. There were rumors that Mayor Kinneman intended to install a sound-deafening fence around Jemison's property, but it had yet to be done.

Jemison was over six feet tall with long black hair and sunken cheek bones. His nails were grimy, and his teeth were rotten, but he never failed to wear a sparkling diamond stud in his nose and flashy clothes that he purchased in the clothing shops on the northern side. His friends were just as disheveled as he was from the neck up, but they wore rags and dusty shoes. Jemison only allowed them the luxury of sleeping in his home, eating his pork and drinking his wine, but he never purchased attire for them. He wanted to be the only one to stand out in his crew.

"I'm sorry, Ursula." A frazzled Bronwyn approached my table with my cup of blackcurrant tea. "You know how it is when they're in here. Your food may not be ready by 7:07."

"Understandable, Bronwyn," I replied. "I may be on the telephone longer than seven minutes this evening anyway. I have more than usual to discuss."

"Do try to take your time. Tabb will prepare your food as soon as these tramps are tended to." She wiped sweat from her forehead and situated the strands of hair falling around her face.

"Hello, dear."
"Ma."

"Good things this week?"

I spoke loudly over the deafening sound of Jemison and his gang, "I retrieved more licorice root for Finley. He said his mother and father are both struggling, and he's unable to work pawning due to his ulcer. His pa has given the managerial duties to his brother, Felkner. I gave Finley some money. I think I'll do some shopping for him next time I'm on the north side."

"Finley is a dear boy and a good friend. I know he must be terribly distraught about his parents, especially since he is unable to tend to them. I pray for healing of his ulcers," Ma replied. "Other news?"

"I made a meat pie for the Teldwin family and mended several of their coats. Fannie Teldwin didn't own a single pair of mittens, and with this recent cold front she was right glad to have a pair of mine."

"Mrs. Teldwin is awful deserving."

"As you suggested, I also visited Pype Tyburn at Mabyn Square."

"Very good, dear! How did you find him?"

"He was quite pleasant." I took a drink of warm tea. "He seems to be doing good things in Mabyn. Were you aware that he is a northerner by birth?"

"I am aware, Ursula."

"Was he banished or did he come here voluntarily? I've never known anyone but you to leave a prosperous life to permanently reside south of the Winnow."

"You'll have to discuss that with him, Ursula. I'm sure he'll be glad to share his story once he's comfortable with you."

"I do not understand what good thing he needs though, Ma. He seems to be doing fine. He appeared clean and well-kempt. I'm unsure where he lives, but I assume he's not struggling. He's able to buy plenty of ingredients to feed the homeless in Mabyn Square. He can't possibly need my money."

"Money is not everyone's need, Ursula. Surely you know that."

"It's most everyone's," I said.

"I implore you to continue seeing Pype. It will become evident what good thing he needs."

"Why can't you just tell me, Ma? You usually tell me when a child covets a toy, when an elderly lady needs tablets, when a family is hungry. Why can't you tell me specifically what Mr. Tyburn requires?"

Ma sighed. "Some things you have to determine on your own, dear daughter."

"Like the homeless man on the corner of 9th and Gwinnett? I've mentioned him to you countless times, yet you've never suggested that I help him beyond dropping a few coins into his cup. I'm certain you know his story, don't you?"

"You're an intelligent woman. You are capable of discerning what help is needed. When you see the homeless man on the corner, with his holey shoes, surely you know replacing them would be a good thing. You do not need me to disclose that, dear. Just as you do not need me to reveal what Pype Tyburn needs— just as you do not need me to reveal what Oden Barmouth needs. What you do not already know, you are surely capable of discovering on your own. I'm merely your guide. I do not have to spell everything out for you, do I?"

"Oden Barmouth is out of the question, Ma. I refuse."

"Forgiveness—"she began.

"You'll be saddened to hear this, Ma, but when I spy Oden Barmouth sitting in his shack without sustenance or heat, I am delighted. I find great amusement at his coldness and hunger. Oden

Barmouth's poverty brings me loads of happiness, Ma! Perhaps that's why I walk down to Hannelore Park– to have the pleasure of seeing him suffer. Isn't that ironic, Ma? My purpose is to do good things for destitute southerners, yet one's destitution brings me joy."

Ma remained silent as Jemison and his raucous friends stepped down from their barstools and slowly walked out the door of the diner, finally leaving the restaurant silent.

"You heard me, yes?" I asked.

"Yes, Ursula, I did."

"Your thoughts are?"

"As I said, dear, you're an intelligent woman. I am sure you can decipher my thoughts."

"Ma, can't you remember what it was like when you were here? Can't you remember the animosity you felt toward Oden Barmouth at one time? I am still here, Ma, and I abhor the man. I do not foresee that ever changing. He robbed me of my father. He robbed you of your husband. How can I forgive that?"

"Ursula," Ma said, "I do remember my former feelings. And I now know my abhorrence of Oden Barmouth did not punish him. It only punished me. The hate that I possessed only made me miserable and bitter. Hate is doing the same for you."

I stood silently at the payphone and twirled the receiver cord around my thin white fingers as the blast of the cold air conditioning wisped my dark hair across my forehead.

"Any other news?" she asked.

"Yes," I said before taking a sip of the berry tea. "I had the pleasure of seeing Mora Sloane again. She was scampering down 3rd. She'd been beaten. Life obviously hasn't been good to her."

"Oh," Ma said. "Mora Sloane! There's another source of hatred for you, innit?"

"Certainly you remember what she put me through, Ma? Certainly you remember the tears and the humiliation she caused. She bullied me relentlessly."

"Indeed I do remember, Ursula, but again, how is your hatred for Mora hurting anyone but you? What good things can you do for Mora Sloane? That's the question you should be asking."

"I can do nothing for that wretched soul." I shook my head.

"Ursula, in our conversation this evening, you've told me the good things you've done this week. But, you've only helped people whom you find deserving! When will you bless the undeserving? When will you love your enemies? That's when your work, your good things, will really matter."

"Ma." I sighed. "It proves difficult."

"If we comprehend and embrace the Most High's forgiveness for us, we can then draw from His infinite provision and begin to love others more fervently and sincerely. Through Him, we can love the unlovable."

"Yes, Ma," I said.

"I do know about the homeless man on the corner of 9th and Gwinnett. Would you like to know about him as well? Would you still help him even if what you learn of his past deems him undeserving in your eyes?"

"I'm unsure, Ma. If what you divulge casts a dark shadow upon him, I will no longer pity him. And, truthfully, I do not want to think differently of him. I'm content believing he's just another unfortunate southerner who warrants kindness."

"And that's why I have not told you secrets that I am privy to, Ursula. That's why I haven't directed you to many who would greatly benefit from good things. You could help so many others if you would just open your heart— if you didn't only deem a select few as worthy of your aid."

I shifted from one canvas shoe to the other and replied, "Tell me then, Ma. Tell me about the man on 9th and Gwinnett."

"If you decide to help him once you know his sins then you've begun to heal the intolerance of your heart."

"Yes," I answered.

"Barton Huxley once lived in a cypress house on Persephone. His wife, Bonnie, became mysteriously ill and suffered for many months." Ma sighed. "He slowly poisoned her, Ursula. Barton Huxley flavored her meals with Macron juice. She burned from the inside out until she took her last ragged breath, and then he buried her in West Dellerby Woods under the cover of night."

"He didn't, Ma?" I gasped.

"Once she was gone, all of Barton's neighbors inquired about Bonnie. He insisted that she'd been captured while trying to escape to Wheatsand. Oh how they pitied Barton Huxley! The elderly ladies provided him with an abundance of charity, meals and even money all the while he lived with his dark secret. He was so well-cared for that he stopped working at the mill. He lived on the generosity of others for many months. He took great pride in a fancy blue suit that he purchased in a northern shop. However, the generosity soon ran out, and Barton needed work. The mill shut down on the very day that he returned to plead for his job.

"Barton attempted to make a wage. He applied as a watchman at the prison and offered his services to the sanitation department and the squad. Barton even begged Mayor Kinneman to allow him to tend to his gardens, but he was denied. Barton Huxley was convinced that he'd been cursed and rebuked by his dead wife from beyond her grave in West Dellerby Woods.

"Soon he was plagued with visions of Bonnie. He was

afflicted with night terrors that left him screaming and soaked in sweat. Eventually Barton Huxley could no longer afford his cypress house, and he's been destined to the corner of 9th and Gwinnett ever since. He's sincerely repentant, but he firmly believes being destitute is just punishment for his sins."

A lone tear fell from the corner of my eye. I mourned the repute that I had associated with the pitiable man who lived simply with a ceramic mug and a cardboard sign.

"I'm unsure how to respond, Ma." I erased the salty tear with the back of my hand.

"We all make mistakes, Ursula. We all fall short yet when we repent, we're all worthy of forgiveness. Who are you to judge the severity of the sin? Is murder worse than thievery? Is thievery worse than refusing to help your brother? Are you the judge of that? Are you the Most High? The Most High over all?"

"No, Ma."

"You're a loving girl, Ursula. You always have been. You were chosen to do good things for those in need because you radiate love. Do not let that love be stifled by your condemnation of others. Those who are truly penitent are deserving of love as well."

"Yes," I said and nodded. "And Papa?"

"You know I can't."

"Yes, Ma."

"Go do good things, dear. I love you. Always."

"Always."

The pulled pork and apple grilled cheese with a side of crisps arrived at my table at 7:18 that evening, delivered by Tabb himself.

"Ursula, I must extend my apologies to you. I can barely

stay afloat when Alcee visits. Those fools leave me in quite a tizzy. I know you prefer your meal directly after your telephone conversation comes to an end. I do sincerely—"

"Tabb, I beg you to stop. There is no inconvenience. Everything looks delicious as always. I thank you."

Tabb showed white teeth that gleamed against his dark skin, nodded his head topped with a frayed hairnet and took long strides back to the kitchen.

As I savored the juicy pork and replayed Ma's words in my mind, the diner's door opened. A gust of cold air and snowy dust entered, followed by the homeless man from the corner of 9th and Gwinnett.

I eyed him carefully as he slowly passed a sleeping Hamill Cooper and approached Bronwyn smoking a cigarette behind the aluminum counter. The floppy soles of his shoes slapped the checkerboard floor.

"Barton." Bronwyn exhaled a puff of smoke. "Tea?"

He nodded without saying a word and pulled the mug from the pocket of his navy suit. He retrieved a coin from the mug, slid it across the counter and traded it for a steaming teacup. Bronwyn said nothing else to him and returned to her cigarette resting in the ashtray. She took another drag, distinguished it and reapplied her lipstick before walking to my booth.

"More tea, Ursula?" she asked and revealed a plum stain on her front teeth.

"No, thank you." I shook my head. "That man? Barton Huxley?"

"The one and only," she answered.

"Do you know much of him?"

"Oh the poor pitiable soul!" she said quietly. "His Bonnie was captured while trying to escape to Wheatsand many years ago.

She'd intended to leave poor Barton because she'd fallen in love with a Wheatsand gentleman that she met over the bridge. I doubt the border patrol took her alive."

"How did he succumb to destitution, Bronwyn?"

"He lost all will to live when his wife was gone. The older ladies tended to him for quite a while, but their open hands eventually closed. The mill shut down, and he was left permanently unemployed. It's an awful gloomy tale. He always seemed such a decent man, not fit for such a destiny."

"Thank you, Bronwyn," I responded before she turned and disappeared behind the kitchen's swinging double doors.

I took the last bite of sandwich and gulped the remainder of tea before standing from the booth. I tossed my money to the table, retrieved Papa's boots and approached Barton Huxley.

"Mr. Huxley?" I asked as he silently shifted his eyes toward me without turning his head. "I'm quite aware of your situation, and I've often noticed the sad state of your footwear. I do hope these will come in handy."

I placed my father's work boots splattered with paint on the red stool next to Barton Huxley and left the diner at 77 7th Street.

FIVE

As snow poured from the sky, I sat at my desk with a teacup of blackcurrant brew and plate of sesame crackers and sighed at the daunting task before me. Garfunkel rested atop my fleece slipper and bathed himself after a breakfast of tuna as I inserted parchment into the typewriter. Suddenly there was a loud banging at my door, and by the rhythm of the pounding knocks, I knew my sister stood on the other side.

If Lolly was in Downforge Alley to pay me a visit so early on a Tuesday morning, it undoubtedly meant that she and Thaddeus had engaged in a quarrel. It also undoubtedly meant that she wanted to raid my cupboards, criticize my lifestyle and sleep on my orange bridgewater-style sofa.

I stood from the wooden chair at my desk, tightened the belt of my heavy green bathrobe and shuffled to the door. A look through the peephole revealed my baby sister anxiously biting her fingernails and shifting from one foot to the other. Before I had fully opened the door, she barged through and began ranting.

"What took so long, Ursula? It isn't as if you have a gentleman caller here that you must hide in a closet or beneath your bureau!" Lolly walked directly to the kitchenette, removed the rye from the bread box and tore off a piece.

"Good morning, Lolly," I said and shut the door. "What has Thaddeus done now?"

"Oh!" she groaned and rested against the counter. "What hasn't he done, Ursula? What hasn't that man done to me over the last fifteen years?"

I sat back at my desk while the uninterested cat continued to clean his paws beneath my chair. I eyed my sister with her hair dyed an unsightly shade of yellow and her tight olive sweater and burgundy corduroy pants clinging to her petite, yet voluptuous, frame.

She stood at the kitchen counter and chewed the bread while slipping scuffed brown boots from her feet. Then she walked to the couch, sat down and covered herself with Ma's patchwork quilt draped over the back.

"Winifred Marcus. That's who he's involved with now, Ursula! Winifred Marcus! Can you conceive Thad and Winifred Marcus in a relationship? Can you possibly conceive it?" she shouted.

I rolled my eyes.

"He claimed he was working late last evening, but I suspected otherwise. I went down to the squad station myself and asked Lieutenant Stevenwill where he was. He confirmed my suspicions. Thaddeus wasn't even scheduled for night watch!"

"Imagine that."

"I wandered downtown for over an hour looking for him. He and Winifred Marcus were playing billiards at Lytton's. Well, I never would have believed!"

"Lolly, I do have plenty of work to get done," I said and nodded at the typewriter.

"Oh," she smirked. "Well, don't mind little old me, Ursula. Don't mind your deceived and heartbroken sister. Would you rather me go back to Valoria and battle with Thad? You know I'll strike first, and he'll strike back. Is that what you want?"

"No."

"Well can't you have pity on me, Ursula? Can't I bunk here until he comes crawling back and begging forgiveness? It's certain that he will."

"It's also certain that you will receive him with open arms, innit, Lolly? Why do you subject yourself to his abuse? Why keep returning?"

Lolly paused and chewed on her berry-colored fingernails before saying, "Because I know nothing else."

Thaddeus Jessop discovered my sister in the schoolyard when she was only 15. He was a 20-year-old patrolman stationed on Gaius Hill, and she was enamored with him from the first time they spoke. When Thad suggested that she leave school early to create a new life with him, she happily obliged.

He whisked her away from our home at the base of Mayor Kinneman's lawn and took her to his flat near Bally's Way. Our mother was incredibly brokenhearted and brought her home on many occasions, but Lolly always ran directly back to Thad. Over the last 15 years, the couple had moved dozens of times until they finally situated in the wooden house on Valoria near the edge of East Dellerby Woods.

Lolly and Thad had a common-law marriage, but his infidelity was a minor offense compared to the other ways he had abused her. She'd had chunks of hair pulled right from her skull and her nose broken twice. His hand had delivered countless blows and bruises and sprains. Knowing she was unable to swim, Thad had once pushed Lolly right into the Winnow after an argument over who ate the last piece of tenderloin.

"You could stay with me, Lolly. Permanently."

Lolly laughed and replied, "Oh, I can't conceive it. Me live here with you, Ursula? I can't possibly conceive it!"

"I forget how different we are," I said and focused on the stack of data entry.

"I'd be forced to drink blackcurrant tea and sleep with that feline every night! Do you even own a radio, Ursula? Have you danced to Gordo Riverdale in over a decade? Oh, how shocked you'd be if I lived here and shook things up."

"The only thing you could do to shock me, Lolly, is to make a wage."

"And what does that mean, dear sister?" Lolly pursed her lips and crossed her arms.

"Nothing." I averted the argument and shook my head.

My sister did love Thaddeus, it was true, but the only reason I could decipher that she remained with him in spite of the physical and emotional abuse was because she was solely dependent on him. She'd never worked a day in her life because Thad provided everything she needed— except true love. I don't know that he'd ever delivered that.

"Will you believe who else I saw at Lytton's last night?"

I shrugged nonchalantly and typed the figures.

"Oden Barmouth," Lolly said as I looked to her. "Oden Barmouth was there leaned against the bar singing gibberish and swaying his glass in the air. I heard he's working for old blind Erskine now. Oden is probably stealing coins out of the register left and right. Erskine can't even see his hand in front of his face, much less keep up with the accounting at the bar."

"He's working for Erskine Lytton? Oden Barmouth is working at the ale house?"

Lolly nodded. "That's what I just said!"

"I walk by his house at times. I see him in his shed by the Winnow, hungry and cold. I try to pity him, but I can't. Is that wrong, Lolly? Should we forgive him?"

"Oden Barmouth deserves whatever hardship he gets," Lolly replied. "He doesn't belong in a shed on the Winnow. He belongs at the bottom of the Winnow."

I nodded in agreement.

"I didn't kill Papa. Oden Barmouth did."

"I know that, Lolly. You do not have to repeat yourself

each time we speak of it."

"I must repeat it. The more I do repeat it, the more it becomes my truth."

Our father, Levon, died when Ma was eight months pregnant with Lolly. He'd gone to Farkas Skett's pawn shop on Persephone to purchase a crib. It was bright cherry with a drop side, and Ma remarked about it every time she passed the store. My sweet papa decided to stop in and purchase it for her as a surprise one summer evening on his way home from work.

A young Oden Barmouth was in Skett's Pawn that evening, lurking in the corner and browsing a set of tools. As Papa conversed with Mr. Skett about the crib in the front window, Oden pulled a revolver. He waved it wildly in the air and demanded that the cash register be opened. Mr. Skett obeyed his orders, but before he handed the money to a frantic Oden, our father decided to play the hero. He tackled Oden Barmouth to the ground and tried to retrieve the gun but was shot in the chest. Oden Barmouth fled.

I was only three, but I remember when Mr. Skett and the squad appeared at our door that evening with the news that would send Ma into early labor. Lolly was born only 3 hours after Papa died. Mr. Skett gave her the crib at no charge.

Ma never wanted Lolly to know the story about our father's demise. Lolly had grown up believing that his heart suddenly failed. It was Mora Sloane, actually, who revealed the truth to my baby sister. It was Mora Sloane who sang in the schoolyard, "He went to buy your bed and he wound up dead!"

As she sang the tune, I balled up my fist and pierced Mora square in the nose. I'll never forget the blood pouring out of her face and the throbbing in my knuckles as she ran away, sobbing. She told Headmaster Anglesey that I had attacked her for no valid reason.

Anglesey led me to the dark and dreary detention hall in the basement of the schoolhouse and instructed me to sit on a concrete bench. She looked down on me and asked for my account of the altercation. I told her, very calmly over the relentless sound of a pipe dripping, that Mora Sloane had heartlessly revealed to my baby sister how our father really perished. Headmaster Anglesey sat beside me on the concrete bench, draped her arm around my shoulder and spoke, "Well, in that case, job well done, Ursula Underwood." I only had to stay in detention for one day instead of three.

Once Lolly knew the truth, she insisted for many years that it was her fault our father was dead. She claimed that if she'd never been conceived, he'd have no reason to be in the pawn shop on that fateful day. Ma repeatedly told her that there was no truth to her dark thoughts, but Lolly lived with an aching regret that still surfaced from time to time.

"Then continue to repeat it if you must, Lolly. Make it your truth," I said.

"And what about your truth, Ursula? Are you finally convinced that what happened to Ma isn't your fault?"

"I'll never be persuaded that it wasn't my fault, Lolly."

"Well, then, you have your burden of shame, and I have mine."

When my eyes stung, my shoulders ached and I could not bear to type another number, I stood from the typewriter. Lolly napped on the couch as snow poured from the dark sky. I covered my sister with the quilt and tossed a cracker down to Garfunkel before slipping on my warm coat and leaving my apartment in Downforge Alley.

Barton Huxley was situated in his familiar spot on the corner of 9th and Gwinnett. As I dropped four coins into the mug setting beside my father's shoes, I noticed the snow resting on the shoulders of his navy suit. The dingy collar of his shirt was raised to help shield his neck from the sharp wind. I pulled the pink scarf from my throat and handed it down to him.

"You may not fancy such a feminine color, Mr. Huxley," I said, "but this might do you some good."

Barton glanced up at me and gently took the scarf from my gloved hands. He nodded quietly and smiled kindly, as usual. I did the same.

Since the conversation with Ma on Sunday, I'd mulled over the notion of helping those who I would usually find undeserving of any good thing. Aside from Oden Barmouth, who I was not yet prepared to aid, another name kept replaying in my head.

Shiloh Pethlen lived inside the 2nd Street Penitentiary all of my life— convicted of murdering his parents when he was a young man. I'd never laid eyes on him, but his reputation was well-known to everyone south of the Nairn Bridge.

I entered the cold, damp jailhouse and walked to the hefty guard dressed in blue and stationed at the front desk. He looked up at me through a cloud of cigarette smoke rolling from the ashtray beside him and asked, "What's your business here?"

"I've come to visit an inmate," I replied. "Shiloh Pethlen."

The guard looked at me quite confused for a moment before showing his chipped teeth through a wide grin. Then he laughed heartily.

"Are you absolutely certain, girl?"

"Yes, Sir," I replied. "I'm absolutely certain. Shiloh Pethlen."

"No one has requested to see Shiloh Pethlen in, well, ever."

"That's terribly sad for Mr. Pethlen, innit? Well, I'd like to be the first then."

"And what business do you have with Shiloh Pethlen?" The guard leaned his elbows on the large desk.

"I'd like to offer him a bit of encouragement. That is all."

"You'd like to encourage a man who killed his parents in cold blood 40 years ago? You condone his behavior?"

"Condone? No, Sir." I shook my head. "I'm just attempting to do something kind for someone undeserving."

"And why is that, girl?"

"My ma requested it of me."

"And who is your ma?"

"Geraldine Underwood," I replied as the guard eyed me warily.

I shoved my hands into my coat's pockets and shifted my weight from one boot to the other. The man took a drag from the cigarette. As the long ash fell to the concrete floor, he picked up the black telephone on his desk.

"Pethlen has a visitor," he said into the receiver. "Yes, Shiloh Pethlen."

He placed the phone back on the desk, stood and tucked the wrinkled tail of his shirt back into his blue pants. Then he nodded to the hallway at the back of the room and motioned for me to follow him.

A musty, mildewed scent overwhelmed me when we entered the dim hallway and passed rows of cells occupied with quiet, mysterious strangers. I kept my head low and only occasionally glanced into the shadowy chambers. Soon I could see a tall, thin guard stationed next to the bars at the end of the hallway. Beside him was a ladder-back chair.

"Pethlen, you've got a visitor," he said when the large guard and I approached him. "You've got ten minutes."

I heard the rattle of chains from inside the cell as the thin watchman pointed to the chair. I sat while he and his large cohort left me there to speak with Shiloh Pethlen.

"Do I know you, Miss?" a hoarse voice asked from the darkness on the opposite side of the bars.

"No, Sir." I shook my head. "I do not think so. My name is Ursula Underwood."

"Underwood? Underwood?" Pethlen pondered. "Any relation to Levon?"

"Levon was my father," I confirmed.

Shiloh walked closer, and I could finally see him in the dim light of a lone yellow bulb hanging above my head. He was a tall and incredibly thin man. His long, lanky arms protruded from his khaki suit, and the chains around his bony wrists were attached to the dark wall behind him. A bushy gray beard covered his face, and definite, deep wrinkles surrounded his glassy blue eyes.

"You don't say? I went to school with your Pa. Good man, he was." He nodded.

"Thank you, Sir."

"I remember the day Oden Barmouth came here." He sat before me on a small round stool. "He was in that cell right behind you. I asked him why he was here. Said he killed a good man. Said the man's name was Levon Underwood. It saddened my heart to hear it."

"Oden Barmouth recognized that my father was a good man then?" I asked, surprised.

"He did. I estimate Oden had no intention of killing anyone that day, especially not a decent man such as your pa. An unlucky event, that was."

"Certainly it was." I exhaled and draped the bottom of my long coat over my knee so that it no longer touched the moldy, damp floor.

"That's why you've paid me a visit then, innit? You want to inquire about your father and Oden Barmouth?"

"No, Sir, I had no knowledge of your relationship with either," I said. "I've come merely to do a good thing for you."

"Oh?" he asked and rested his bony elbows on his knees. The chains hanging from his wrists clinked against the floor. "And what good thing is that, Underwood?"

"That's what you will have to tell me. What do you need, Mr. Pethlen?"

"What do *I* need, girl? What do *I* need?" His gray beard parted in a smile and revealed dark teeth.

"What can I do to encourage you, Mr. Pethlen? Bring you a special meal? A certain book? Are those luxuries even allowed here?"

"What's this all about?" He crossed his thin legs.

"Well," I said and gulped, "my ma encourages me to do good things for those in need. Up until now, I've been quite content in performing noble tasks for those who I find to be deserving of them. My ma pointed out something that I'm realizing may be of importance, however."

"Ma's have a good way of doing that," he interrupted.

"She pointed out that I have no qualms about helping those who I fit deserving, which is all fine and well, but I've yet to help anyone who I judge harshly for their blatant sin."

"Sinners like me, then?" he asked.

"Yes, Sir."

"Then you know why I'm in here, Underwood?"

"Everyone knows, Mr. Pethlen. It's not a very vast place

here south of the Winnow. Most criminals are infamously popular."

He sighed. "Underwood, I'm not the same boy who killed his parents 40 years ago. Look upon me. I'm an old man now. I've been in this jail cell for the majority of my life. That's had a profound impact on me."

"You do regret what you did then?"

"Every second of my life, I do, but I've made peace with it. My parents come to me here, you know?"

"They do?" I shook my head.

"That they do. They visit me here often. I see them in a mist as they hover right above my cot there, see? My mother forgives me. She takes every opportunity to tell me that. And my father, well, he's finally come around. They do excuse me, and I've finally excused myself."

"May I ask why you did it?" I shifted in the uncomfortable chair.

"I'm not certain of that, Underwood. I have had many years to sit in this prison and ponder that very question, but I'm still not certain. Rage, I suppose. Rage ruled my life back then." He ran his wrinkled hands through his beard. "Rage is an evil thing, it is. It never produces righteousness."

"Your parents did not mistreat you then?"

"No," he scoffed. "I was born to good people. I grew up in a warm and loving home near Gaius Hill. I had no valid reason to commit such wickedness. Father didn't throw me around. Mother didn't yell, yet I was still so full of anger and darkness. But my parents have forgiven me, as well as the Most High, and that is the only good thing I'd ever covet, Underwood. That's the only good thing I need, and I've received it."

"Right then."

"You deem Oden Barmouth undeserving, I suppose?"

"That I do," I answered.

"Your mother? Does she insist that you do good things for him?"

"It would please her very much. However, I'm not ready to do any noble thing for the man who murdered my father."

"Did it surprise you when I said Oden felt repentance for taking Levon's life?"

"I've painted quite the picture of Oden Barmouth in my head, Mr. Pethlen, and I don't visualize an atoned man. I only visualize a heartless murderer."

"Would it persuade you to do good things for Oden if I told you that he cried himself to sleep each night that he was in that cell?"

"I'm not sure, Mr. Pethlen."

"Your mother asks you to help him so I assume she has forgiven him, Underwood? And I'm certain your father has pardoned Oden."

"Yes, my mother has forgiven Oden Barmouth, and I suppose my father has, as well, but it is easier for the dead to forgive than the living, Mr. Pethlen."

"That may be accurate, Underwood, but the most curing, gratifying and beneficial things are challenging."

"You sound like Ma," I said and looked to the floor.

"I see an internal struggle here, Underwood. I see a young woman purposed to be salt and light among the dark and dismal. But if salt has no taste, what good is it? Lamps do not belong under baskets, do they? No! They belong on stands to give light to all in the house. Your light is purposed to shine before others, all others, so that they may see your good works and give glory to the Most High."

I nodded.

"I see a young woman who, at the advice of her wise mother, wants her purpose to come to fruition, but she's following her flesh. Your spirit tells you to bless all, Underwood, but your flesh tells you to do only what is predictable— to love your neighbor and loathe your enemy. Don't do what is predictable, Underwood. You'll benefit if you don't merely do what is predictable. If you only love those who love you, what's the reward in that?"

"Mr. Pethlen, I came to do a good thing and encourage you, yet I perceive you're the one doing a good thing for me."

He chuckled and shook his head. "You've done more good for me today than you'll ever know, Underwood. You've given me a glimpse of the outside world, and I'm pleased to see that salt and light remain in people like you."

When I stepped out of the jail, the earlier snow had left a thick dusting on the cobblestone streets. I quickly walked west with my head down to escape the brutal wind.

I felt somewhat refreshed as I scurried past a sleeping Barton Huxley— wrapped in my scarf, wearing my father's shoes and blanketed by parchment. A murderer's words of inspiration had left me refreshed, which only days ago I would've never deemed possible. I thought of Pethlen's claim that Oden Barmouth was repentant for my father's death as I unlocked my door to find Garfunkel sleeping on the couch next to a note.

UU, Thad came for me. LU

"What will we do with foolish Lolly, Garfunkel?" I asked the cat as he stretched and looked up at me to feed him.

SIX

While leaned against a faulty column in the coliseum, I watched Pype Tyburn pour bubbling soup into the vagrants' cardboard bowls. When the line lessened, he walked toward me, both his shaggy hair and his gray apron blowing in the bitter wind.

"Ms. Underwood." He presented a helping to me.

"I couldn't," I said and shook my head. "I have plenty of food at home."

"Please." He pressed the steaming bowl into my gloved hands. "Rest assured that a portion can be spared for you."

"But I–"

"It is made with the finest ingredients, and it's my mother's own recipe. I'll be offended if you don't have it."

I nodded and reluctantly took the steaming broth from him.

"Shall I join you while you eat?" he asked.

"That would be quite fine," I replied. "I'll sit over here–"

"No such thing," he said. "My flat is only a two minute walk to 2nd Street. You'll have your soup there where it's warm."

"I do not want to drag you away from your station."

"The rush is over, I'm due for a break, and Mr. Gunnar is somewhat capable of handling things while I'm gone."

I silently followed Pype Tyburn through the square crowded with the displaced gulping their lunch. I slowed when a small girl with sad eyes and a dirty face looked up at me from her mother's knees as she shoveled the chowder into her mouth.

"Did you know Bally?" Pype interrupted my stare.

"No," I said and quickly shuffled to catch up with him. "I do remember the sound of the fire engines and the black smolder that clouded the entire town. Ash rained down everywhere– even on the schoolhouse on Gaius Hill."

"Poor Chap," Pype said as we crossed the cobblestone

street and stepped over the charred brick piled along the sidewalk.

We walked silently, our breath forming puffs of smoke in the frosty air. The warmth of the soup grazed my face, and I could hardly wait to have a taste of what appeared to be corn and coconut.

"I'm right here then." Pype nodded to the gray apartment building towering on the corner of 2nd and Gwinnett, directly across from the penitentiary where I had visited Shiloh Pethlen the night before.

"Did you know Rosella Darkmoor? She was on the second floor of this building. She crossed over last fall."

"Oh, yes," Pype said. "She had those shepherd dogs that howled like wolves every time it thundered. They kept me awake many nights in the spring. She seemed a sweet woman though."

"Very kind, she was. She was a dear friend of my mother's."

We walked through the heavy front door of the building and up two sets of creaky wooden stairs to the first beige door on the left. Pype pulled a lone key from the pocket of his apron and jangled it in the lock. It proved difficult, but it finally turned. He motioned for me to enter first.

"Pardon the mess," he said. "I did not expect company today."

I looked around the pristine flat and asked, "What mess do you speak of?"

He laughed. "I'll admit that I'm a bit fanatical about cleanliness. I try to leave things in disarray. I really do, but it never sets well with me. I purposely left an empty teacup on my table for fifteen minutes, and it nearly drove me mad! Every time I glanced at that cup, I perspired. I just cannot endure things being out of place."

"There are worse faults to have."

"Please, sit down." He motioned to the oversized moss-colored sofa in the middle of the living room. "I do not have a proper eating area, as you can see, but the couch does serve many purposes. Just refrain from spilling anything on the cushions. As you can imagine, stains make me a bit skittish. It's comical the lengths I'll go to in order to keep my apron clean every day."

I smiled, sat on the comfortable couch and carefully placed my lunch on the coffee table made of wide Runyon planks. I slipped out of my coat and tossed it over the back of the sofa.

"I'll take that!" Pype scooped it up before I could get my hands off of it.

"Yes, you really are a stickler for proper organization, aren't you?" I watched him hang my wool coat and his tidy apron on the hooks of the hall tree next to his door.

"Afraid so," he answered and smiled. "Shall I boil you some water? Herbal tea perhaps?"

"The soup'll be right fine." I retrieved the bowl from the table and took a sip. It was delicious corn and coconut as I had suspected.

Pype sat across from me in a wide plaid chair and pulled a cigar from the drawer of the small table next to him.

"You mind my smoke?" he asked as I shook my head. "I only have one cigar a day; half after lunch and half before bed. I've been doing that for years, just like my pa."

Pype struck a match along the bottom of his gray lace-up boot, put the flame to the cigar and sucked until fire took over the end and smoke soon surrounded his head. I eyed the spotless apartment with its fine furnishings and khaki-colored walls before finally fixing my attention on a large family portrait near the front window— matted in the same shade of green as the couch and framed stylishly. I quickly spotted tall, thin Pype in the right corner of the photo.

"How do you react if ash accidentally falls to the floor?" I suddenly shifted my eyes down to him and nodded to the cigar.

"Oh, you don't bloody want to know, now do you? I pull up the rug and take it outside and beat it for half an hour if I have to! Quite obsessive, innit?"

"Possibly," I answered after taking another slurp of the broth. "However, I'd loads rather lean that way instead of the opposite. Cleanliness is a virtue. Squalor is not."

He smiled. "You're enjoying the soup then?"

"It's divine. I have not enjoyed corn and coconut since I was a little girl. Our old neighbor, Mrs. Sabille, always brought over a batch when my sister Lolly or I was sick. I looked forward to being ill just so I could get a bowl of it. I think this might top hers!"

"My mother's recipe, that is. I don't like to boast, but I do find it to be quite tasty. The homeless request it often. I know they'd be grateful for a run-of-the-mill vegetable or potato, but I do try to grant their requests when I'm able."

"Tell me about that," I said. "Tell me how your mission began."

"There's not much to tell really." He blew rings of smoke from his mouth. "I grew up north of the Winnow, and now I live south."

"And how many fellows can say that?" I smiled. "There is a story there. If you do not want to share it with me, it's quite alright, but do not say there is not much to tell!"

He chuckled. "That picture behind me. The one you were staring at a moment ago?"

I felt my face blush as I nodded and placed the empty bowl

on my lap.

"On the bottom row from left to right— that's my mother, Delia, my father, Proctor, and my youngest sister, Glennis. That attractive animal you see there front and center is my beloved Aiko. He was my most cherished friend. I have no doubt that if I walked up to him right this moment that he'd remember me well. He'd have me pinned to the floor, licking my face! It would be a memorable reunion!"

I looked at the yellow Labrador poised beautifully at the feet of the distinguished man Pype named as his father.

"You know where everyone is placed in the portrait without even looking at it?" I asked as he nodded. "You've studied it much then?"

"On the top row is my brother-in-law, Tavish, in the middle is his wife and my older sister, Tegwen, and then there's me. My hair was shorter then, but my height certainly wasn't! That was taken three years and three months ago."

"It's a fine looking family," I said and placed the bowl on the coffee table. I noticed the sudden distraught look on Pype's face. "Shall I put the bowl in the trash bin?"

"I'll take it," he offered.

"No, no." I shook my head and stood. "The bin?"

"It's in the kitchen cupboard below the sink."

I left the tidy living room and walked only a few steps to the equally spotless kitchen and tossed the cardboard bowl into the garbage. I noticed the sparkling dishes stacked perfectly behind a glass cupboard door and the shine on the silver faucet.

"Lovely kitchen," I said and walked back to the couch. "It deems sterile enough for an operation."

"For me there's no other option." He laughed.

"You miss them greatly then?" I sat down and looked back

to the portrait of the northern family dressed in dapper suits and ball gowns.

"Terribly, especially my Aiko, but I did what I felt was the right thing to do. I came here to live with real purpose. I've a servant's heart. That's what my mother always said anyway."

"They approved of your decision to come here?"

"Not especially." He exhaled more of the sweet-scented smoke. "My father was keenly against it. My mother always tends to err on the same side as my father, although she's not as vocal as he. My sisters were the most understanding I suppose."

"Your sisters look quite charming."

"They are. They really are. I miss them nearly as much as the Labrador."

"What was the definitive reason you came downtown? To help people, I know, but I'm curious what—"

"Two little girls," Pype interrupted and stared at the cigar smoldering in his hand. "Two little girls were begging the grocer for bread. I stood on the stoop of my father's jewelry store and watched Mr. Rendwick turn them away because they were a few coins short. He turned them away, not caring that they were thin as rails or that they had an inch of dirt beneath their fingernails. I walked over and paid for the bread, along with lamb and veal, and I spoke to the children. They said the dirt beneath their nails was the product of digging for potatoes. They said they hadn't eaten in days, and their mother was dying downtown. They'd walked across the bridge, alone, just for a loaf of bread. I asked if they had bread on the south side, and they said their bakery had shut down."

"I remember that well," I said. "Poor Ms. Purvis' husband had just died, and she was so overcome with grief that she closed her business for several months. She didn't go to the north side once in all that time to purchase yeast. We all stocked up on as much bread as we could when we went north."

"Those two little girls," Pype mumbled and shook his head. "They changed me that day, and I suddenly felt very guilty living north of the Winnow. I had been so spoiled. My sisters and mother wore bulbous jewels, and my father played Rugby for leisure, and I'd attended the finest schools all while little girls were digging for potatoes and begging for bread only a few miles away. I could not sleep at night because of that guilt. I came south to sleep again."

"And you were forced to leave all of your wealth behind? How do you afford ingredients like coconut? How do you manage to keep the soup kitchen running?"

"See, that's the complex part." Pype distinguished the half-smoked cigar in the ashtray on his lap. Then he pulled a towel from the drawer next to him, wiped out the ashtray and concealed it all back in the drawer. "Of course I'm not allowed to visit my family on my allotted trips north or I'll absolutely be forbidden to ever cross the Nairn Bridge again. But my eldest sister, Tegwen, leaves letters and sums of money behind a whitewashed brick with a chipped edge in Kendrew Alley. The letters give me great peace of mind that my family, and my dog, is doing well. The money allows me to purchase ingredients for soup and to pay for this flat. Of course if that knowledge were to become common, my sister would be severely punished."

"Yet you tell me?" I asked, surprised. "You do not know me, Pype Tyburn. I could very well give this information to the northern squad and have you all done for."

He shook his head. "I oughtn't to believe that for a moment! As my mother would say, you've a servant's heart as well. It's evident."

I relaxed into the couch and sighed. "See, there was loads of a story to tell, wasn't it?"

"I estimate there's plenty more if you're interested."

"I estimate any tale about northern deserters is interesting."

"My sister is Mrs. Tegwen Dunbryll. Her husband, Tavish, is the son of the northern mayor."

"No!" My eyes widened. "You're related by marriage to the very people who killed so many in the Cronin Civil War? The very people who want nothing more than to annihilate anyone residing south of the Winnow? And now you're here aiding southerners?"

"It's a riot, innit?" Pype laughed. "Although you'd be very surprised to know that my brother-in-law, Tavish, is quite sympathetic to southerners. Oh, his father doesn't know or he'd likely have him beheaded, but Tegwen mentions often in her letters how her husband longs to see peace between the banks of the river. He longs for things to be as they were in the time of Dessick Mabyn."

I shook my head in disbelief and said, "Your brother-in-law, does he know the lengths his wife goes to help her brother?"

"He does. He approves. As I said, he's sympathetic to my cause. I find great hope in Tavish being Shaw Dunbryll's heir."

I leaned forward on the couch. "There's hope for reconciliation in our lifetime?"

"That there is, Ursula."

SEVEN

As I crossed the Nairn Bridge, the bitter wind gusted and large, choppy waves overtook the usually calm Winnow River. Through the iron slats beneath my boots, I watched the water rage as I shifted my hefty canvas bag of drawing supplies from one shoulder to the other. I situated it often on the twelve-minute trek north.

The line to sign the registry in Algirdis Square was quite lengthy, as it was most Saturdays. I lightly bounced up and down to keep my watery blood flowing through my chilled veins while I waited in the harsh gale. I feared the weather would keep people away from the boardwalk and leave me no chance of selling a caricature.

When it was finally my turn to sign the leather-bound ledger that set on a podium beneath the decorative and elaborate structure of Dessick Mabyn, my frozen fingers could barely maneuver the pen. Any illegible signature was cause for great concern, so I took my time to carefully print:
U R S U L A U N D E R W O O D – W O R K A N D S H O P 9:12 A M

Despite the frosty wind, crowds of people grazed the square and congested Whishart Avenue. The shops were bustling, and the smell of freshly-baked bread and steaming pork wafted on the cold air. It was easy to recognize which side of the river each person lived on. The flashy, expensive clothing and hats revealed a northern address, and those dressed plainly obviously hailed from the south. Although we looked so different, northerners and southerners walked alongside one another with shopping bags in their hands.

A large lady with fiery red hair caught my attention as I turned from Whishart Avenue and stepped onto the wooden boardwalk. She was the spitting image of the woman who shouted at my mother in the library of her Wheatsand manor 26 years ago.

She stopped abruptly and parted a pack of people to light a brown cigarillo before tossing the used match to the street. Smoke circled her ruby hair topped by a fuchsia hat adorned with a golden feather. She didn't notice me standing there, gawking at her, and she proceeded down the street and was soon lost in the crowd. I had only seen hair that shade on my grandmother's head, and I was certain the woman with the golden feather was my relation.

I halted at an empty spot on the boardwalk between Swann Rexlee's face-painting station and Dennison Thorburn's sausage and pepper cart. Swann and Dennison were both southerners whom I often saw on the boardwalk. Swann was a mousy and quiet young girl with long and paper-thin white bangs concealing most of her face. Dennison was hefty with a beard concealing most of his. The only time I had ever eaten from his cart, my sausage sandwich contained wiry hairs that had shed from his face. I opted not to partake again.

"Morning, Ursula," Dennison said while placing sausages on the stainless steel cooking rollers.

"Dennison." I pulled the heavy canvas sack from my shoulder and rested it on the boardwalk.

"Seems to be a good crowd out and about today, innit? They must be preparing for the storm."

"Storm?" I asked and pulled a small folding stool from the bag.

"Oh yes, Ursula. There's a blizzard coming! It ought to arrive tonight. Best load up on foodstuffs while you're here. I'll be glad to pack you some sausages to take back over the bridge."

"That's quite nice, Dennison, but I'll make do. I knew

inclement weather was brewing but had no idea it'd be a blizzard."

"I contemplated not coming today, but nothing makes northerners hungry like shopping! I suspect to make quite the loot today on sausages. The elite will shop for snow shovels and new mittens while their bored children whine at their ankles, so they'll send the youngsters down here for face paints and caricatures! When the parents come to retrieve them, they'll have their fill of sausage and peppers, and we'll all make quite the loot! I just hope the northern squad doesn't take our earnings from us this time!" Dennison hummed.

"I hope you're correct, Dennison," I said as I sat on the stool and pulled colored pencils and my sketch pad from the bag.

The angry river loudly sloshed against the wooden pillars of the boardwalk as Dennison's theory proved true. Parents sent their complaining children from the boutiques and bakeries on Whishart Avenue to be entertained by us vendors on the boardwalk. They stopped first for cotton candy at Potter White's stand and then skipped over to Swann. She often quietly asked them to wipe the pink spun sugar from their mouths before she painted them as bears and fairies.

A little girl with short, dark hair and freckles shifted her weight from one glittered shoe to the other and impatiently waited her turn in Swann's line. She finally saw me sitting on the stool, alone, with my own colors set out before me.

"You paint faces, as well?" She approached me.

"I draw caricatures," I answered.

"And what are character chairs?"

I smiled. "Caricatures are an exaggerated portrait. Would you like to see an example?"

She nodded and pulled her purple toboggan hat down over her ears while I searched in the large bag. I retrieved a caricature that I'd drawn of Lolly many years ago and handed it to her.

"That's funny!" She laughed. "The nose is so big! And the body is so small!"

"Yes. That's my sister." I smiled. "Quite humorous, innit?"

"I want one! You can draw me like that?"

"I can." I nodded as she pulled coins from her pocket and dropped them into my earthenware jar. I unfolded another small stool and placed it in front of me.

"May I leave my bonnet on?" she asked and sat down.

"Yes, I can sketch your bonnet if you'd like."

"Yes, I'd like that. I'll hang this in my room for everyone to see. My brother will want one next time we make the journey to the boardwalk!"

"You're not from the north side?" I sketched on my pad.

"I'm from Wheatsand. My ma and I came today to visit friends and shop before the storm. We're going to get piles of snow! Ma says I won't have to go to the schoolhouse for days! She bought me a new fleece coat, as well. It's purple to match my bonnet. I can hardly wait to wear it!" she squealed.

"A purple fleece coat sounds quite lovely," I said. "What's your name?"

"Rupalia! Rupalia Rollo."

"A lovely coat for a lovely name."

"You'll give me a big nose?"

"The biggest."

I sketched the little girl's dark eyes and exaggerated the freckles on her cheeks and over-sized nose. I topped her cocoa-colored hair with a particularly small purple hat and drew her in the fleece coat that she'd described instead of the teal one that she was wearing.

"May I see?" she impatiently asked.

"Not quite yet." I bit my lip and shaded in the coat with my violet pencil.

"This is going to be so funny!" She laughed. "Do you ever draw in Wheatsand? You could come and draw all of my friends!"

"I have only been to Wheatsand once when I was about your age."

"Oh, Wheatsand is lovely. You should visit!" She smiled. "Lady Abertha and my mother are dear friends. Lady Abertha has a Clydesdale. He's 18 hands, and I'm the only one he'll let ride him!"

"He sounds like a marvelous creature."

"You must come see him, too! Have you drawn animals before? Oh, he'd be a sight to sketch!"

"I live south of here, Rupalia. I'm not permitted to visit your home."

"Not permitted? It's merely a short tram ride through Dellerby Woods."

I didn't feel it was my obligation to explain segregation and civil war to a Wheatsand child, so I remained silent and focused on the sketch.

"Rupalia!" a voice carried on the bitter gust. "Where've you been? How much time does face painting require?"

I looked up from my drawing pad to see the large woman with the flaming hair approaching us.

"Ma-ma, I'm having a character chair drawn! It's going to be so humorous!"

"A what?" she asked and glanced down at me.

"A caricature," I said and held the sketch up for the red-head to see.

"Oh!" She giggled. "I've never seen such! Rupalia, it favors you and yet it doesn't! Isn't it odd?"

"It's a riot, innit, Ma-ma?"

"Quite so!" She bobbed her head. "We'll have to bring Carney here to have his portrait drawn, won't we?"

"He'd like that," Rupalia agreed.

I scribbled gray lines behind Rupalia to signify the gusting wind and signed the bottom with a single U. Then I placed the blowing sheet in the child's small hands.

"You drew the purple coat! Ma-ma, she drew my new purple coat!" Rupalia laughed.

"I quite love it." Her mother smiled. "It's very good work indeed."

"Thank you," I said.

"Do you hire out for parties? My son, Carney, would much love for you to attend his birthday celebration and sketch his friends. Name your price!"

Embarrassed, I felt my cheeks turn a warm shade of crimson. "I'm flattered, Miss, but I live south."

"Oh." Her face suddenly soured as she eyed my ordinary wool coat and black boots. "Well, thank you for your time. Come, Rupalia."

"Are you a relation of Ursula Renfrew?" I blurted as the young girl stood and joined her mother's side.

"I beg your pardon?" She turned to me.

"You remind me of Ursula Renfrew. You know of her?"

"I do," she paused. "The better question is how do *you* know of her?"

I shrugged, unsure how to answer. "She knew my mother."

The woman with the fiery red hair gawked at me silently as the lapel of her bright coat and the feather in her fuchsia hat furiously flapped in the windstorm.

"And your mother is?"

"Geraldine." I gulped as she peered down at me sitting on the stool. "Geraldine Renfrew, Ursula's oldest daughter. I am Ursula's granddaughter."

She glared at me for a moment before she abruptly grabbed Rupalia's arm, turned and marched away.

"Refer them here, Ursula!" Dennison called from his sausage and pepper cart. "Don't let them go just yet! Refer them here!"

While sitting frozen on the stool for nearly an hour, I came to the conclusion that the red-headed woman must have been my Aunt Marigold's daughter. Marigold was my mother's older sister and was vehemently angry with Ma for deserting the family to live with a southern painter. Ma had once told me that her sister's last words to her were, "You are now dead to me."

Odds were that Marigold had never spoken of her younger sister to her daughter with the burning hair. Odds were that a complex conversation would ensue between the redhead and Aunt Marigold when she reached Wheatsand.

When I could no longer withstand the cold wind gusting off the water, I folded the small stools and placed them in the canvas bag along with my sketch pad and colored pencils. I said goodbye to Swann and Dennison and walked to Whishart Avenue.

In front of the market, a southern man was being beaten by a northern official in a starched plum uniform— for what I did not know. The poor southerner, dressed in rags, leaned against the front of the market. Blood trickled from his nose as the northerner pounded him repetitively. People carried on about their business, not pausing for a moment. It was incredibly mundane to see this violence against southerners taking place on northern streets.

I walked past the beating, dodged into the market and

quickly spent the money I'd earned from Rupalia's portrait along with my paycheck for the week's data entry. I purchased fresh fish, vegetables, canned foods and several jugs of sparkling water. I also stocked up on cabbage for Finley's ulcer and spoiled him with a small tin of spiced tea. While waiting to pay, I overheard a man call the grocer by his name. I recollected Pype's tale of the two little girls who had begged this man, Rendwick, for bread.

Rendwick was mannerly when I paid him for the food, and I could not envision him as the kind to turn away two starving children. However, failure to compensate what was owed did bring out dire wickedness in people.

I placed the grocery sacks into the canvas bag with my drawing supplies and heaved all of it over my aching shoulder. I tightly cinched the bag closed and stepped into the cold while noticing the bloodied man had been carried away. I hesitated before I crossed the busy street where Tyburn's Trinkets was located.

A bell on the cherry door jingled when I entered. The store was empty with the exception of a man standing behind a glass case showcasing sparkling, luxurious rings and watches. He was tall and broad-shouldered and wore a loupe on his eyeglasses. I recognized him from the matted portrait that was displayed in Pype's home. It was certainly his handsome father.

"Hello, Miss." He eyed my plain, dark clothes and mustered a small smile. "What do you fancy today?"

"Hello. I'm just browsing."

"Very well." He sighed.

Mr. Tyburn was well aware that I, a southerner, was unable to afford such extravagant jewels. He watched me warily as if I were going to flash a weapon and demand that he give me rubies and the platinum dinner ring showcased on the center display. I ignored him, though, and slowly made my way around the store, pausing to marvel at the gems before finally stopping before him.

"Did you fancy anything?" he asked.

"I fancy quite much." I ran my finger along the glass case. "But you're mindful that I'm from the south, Mr. Tyburn. I could not even afford the felt boxes which house such lavish rings."

He pursed his lips and removed his glasses. "And what are you doing here then, girl?"

I locked eyes with those that resembled Pype's and said, "Your son is doing good things, Mr. Tyburn. You oughtn't to be dismayed at his decision to go south. In fact, you ought to be quite proud of him."

He stared at me silently, mouth slightly agape.

"He's doing good things," I repeated and walked out the door, the bell echoing behind me.

The pack hanging from my shoulder seemed to get heavier with every moment I spent waiting to sign the exit registry. The rope handle dug into my gloves and burned my palms. I shifted it from one side to the other and exhaled warm puffs of breath.

"He's rather sick," I overheard a southern woman with short, brown curls say to the bony man standing beside her.

"Hearsay, Wenda. Hearsay," the skinny man retorted and shook his head.

"Hearsay from a northerner! The northerners must know the facts!"

"Rubbish," he scoffed.

"Griffith, the man who said Mayor Dunbryll is on his death bed looked to be someone of importance! Surely he knows actualities!"

"Pardon me," I interrupted and turned to face them. "What's this you say?"

The woman glanced left and right before she leaned in closely and spoke softly, "I overheard a northern man tell his wife at the apothecary that Dunbryll is ill. He spoke it quietly, but I undoubtedly heard it. I'm keen in that sense. I can hear Griffith break wind all the way down on Gwinnett if I try hard enough!" She grinned.

"Ill?" I shifted the weighty sack from my shoulder to the cobblestone street.

"Not too hard to believe, though, innit? He's quite advanced in years. Griffith here thinks the man is immortal," she smirked.

"He's got the finest physicians in the land," Griffith spoke. "They'll keep him ticking for a long time to come. You'll see."

She rolled her eyes at her husband and looked to me. "You think it'll change when Dunbryll is long gone? Will it worsen? Will the allotted visits cease? Will they close up Ms. Purvis' shop and our other few luxuries as they've threatened to do before? Will the new heir annihilate us all? I loathe the old crow, but I fear what will happen when his time is done! A young, vicious ruler is more threatening than an old one!" A look of worry covered Wenda's round face.

"Surely not. I pray surely not."

EIGHT

From my window in Downforge Alley, I watched the snow steadily pour from the night sky. It piled along the cobblestone streets and formed tall drifts against the apartment buildings across from mine. I immediately thought of the homeless population shielded only with newsprint and unstable tarpaulins that would eventually cave with the weight of the slush.

After finishing a cup of warm tea, I put my wool coat over my flannel nightgown and slipped my socked feet into the brown galoshes that I hadn't worn since the last blizzard years ago. I covered my head with my warmest knit hat, left my apartment and descended the stairs of my building.

The relentless snowfall barely allowed me to see my own hand in front of my face as I struggled to sludge through the piles on the sidewalk. I finally reached the corner of 9th and Gwinnett. Barton Huxley was there. His face was covered with the cardboard sign that he held each day, and his body was shielded with my scarf and thin sheets of paper.

"Mr. Huxley?" I bent down to shake his arm.

He slowly removed the sign from his face and looked up at me with a snow-dusted mustache and blue lips.

"Mr. Huxley, come with me, alright?" I pulled him by his armpit and helped him to his feet. "Come with me."

We shuffled down the slippery sidewalk, the few coins in his coat pocket jingling and my father's heavy boots leaving firm prints in the snow. He kept his head down and remained silent with the exception of his teeth chattering.

We climbed the creaky wooden stairs of my building as each step echoed throughout the foyer. I unlocked the door of my apartment and motioned for him to go in first. Instead he bent down to unlace my father's wet work boots and remove them from his feet. He revealed stained and holey socks.

"That's very kind, Mr. Huxley. You can leave them out here in the hallway. Only Ms. Finglo and I reside on this floor, and she has no need for a pair of men's work boots. They'll be safe."

I put my dripping galoshes beside my father's old shoes, and we both went inside my warm apartment. Barton stood there, awkwardly and silently, as snow dripped from his shoulders and formed a small puddle on the parquet floor. He noticed the water and looked up at me, ashamed.

"It's no worry," I said as I reached for a plaid towel on my kitchen counter. "No worry at all, Mr. Huxley. Why don't you take off your coat and hang it there on the hook by the door where it can dry?"

He obeyed my request while I mopped the slush and tossed the towel to the kitchen basin. I removed my coat and bit my lip, unsure what I should say to this man who probably hadn't been under a roof in ten years or more.

"Have a seat, please." I motioned to the couch. "I'll fix you a cup of tea if you'd like? Blackcurrant?"

He nodded kindly and slowly made his way to the sofa. I began preparing the tea, and although his back was to me, I noticed his reflection in the window where Garfunkel was sleeping. Barton Huxley was grinning with gratitude.

As the tea warmed on the stove, I stoked the ash and half-burned logs in the living room fireplace. Barton Huxley watched me quietly with his frozen hands stretched toward the flame.

"Here you go." I finally handed him the steaming teacup before sliding Garfunkel to the side and sitting in the chilly wooden windowsill.

Barton sat rigid and stiff on the edge of the sofa and slurped his drink as I said, "I do wish you'd relax, Mr. Huxley. Lean into the sofa. It's quite comfortable. It sets right well."

He slowly rested against my mother's quilt draped on the back and nodded once again, another small grin forming beneath his mustache.

"I do not believe we've been formally introduced, Mr. Huxley. My name is Ursula Underwood. I'm the one who gave you the shoes and the scarf," I paused and blushed. "Oh, listen to me. As if I'm begging for praise. You know very well what I've given you. I do not know why I deemed to repeat it. That's quite haughty of me. I apologize."

His deep blue eyes peered at me above the teacup.

"I do not know if I should say this, Mr. Huxley, but as you have probably realized, I often speak things that aren't required." I pet the purring cat resting against my thigh. "I'm intimately aware of your situation. I hope you understand what I mean by that."

He slowly shook his greasy head to signal that he did not comprehend.

"Well," I hesitated. "I'm aware of the situation with your wife, Bonnie. I'm aware of the practicalities of the situation, I do mean."

He remained silent.

"Mr. Huxley." I flinched uneasy. "I know that your wife is buried in West Dellerby Woods…by your own hand." I searched his stunned face. "Yet I want you to know that I do not fear you. I do, in fact, wish to help by offering my sofa to you this evening. I tell you this only because I know that you do not feel deserving of such gratitude, and I do not want you to slip away into the blizzard this evening as recompense for your sins, Mr. Huxley. I'm aware of your sins. I do opt to help anyway. I want you to know that you're worthy of forgiveness, Mr. Huxley. That is all."

We stared at one another for what seemed like an eternity until Barton Huxley's bright blue eyes glazed over. He quickly broke our stare before the first tear streamed down his cheek. Then he slowly leaned forward to place the teacup on the coffee table.

"I apologize, Mr. Huxley." I looked down to Garfunkel.

"No." His quiet and gravelly voice startled me. "There's no apology necessary. How did you know? Bonnie came to you in a dream, did she? That's it, innit?"

I shook my head. "No, Sir. My mother, Geraldine Underwood, told me."

"I see." He nodded. "She knows many things?"

"Yes," I said. "I only recently learned your history. My ma only revealed it to help grow me. She told me so that I would be forced with the decision to help someone who I deemed unworthy. She showed me how judgmental I've been."

"I see," he repeated.

"However, this truly is more about you than me, Mr. Huxley. I do want to help you. I would like for you to accept my offer to stay here this evening. I cannot rest knowing you're unsheltered in the snowstorm."

"I do not deserve your kindness. I do not deserve your shoes or scarf or the coins you toss into my cup, and I certainly do not deserve your shelter."

"I would usually agree with you, Mr. Huxley, but if you're repentant, you deserve all of those things. I'd like to offer them."

"You're the first to do anything kind for me in years. I haven't sat by a fire since the widows on Persephone cared for me. I took such advantage of them."

"Yes." I nodded.

"I thought, perhaps, that Bonnie had lifted the curse. When you left the painter's boots for me in the diner, I surely thought it was a sign that she'd forgiven me and possibly prompted you, through a dream or a vision, to reach out."

"You truly believe your wife cursed you from beyond the grave?"

"I'm quite certain," he answered. "She came to me often in terribly horrific dreams. She made it evident that I'd suffer for what I'd done, but she hasn't visited me in a long time now. It leaves me confused, but maybe there's peace to be found in that. Maybe she's forgiven me now. Maybe the Most High has forgiven me."

"May I ask why, Mr. Huxley? Why you took her life?"

He suddenly dropped his tired face into the palms of his dirty hands. I could see the tears leak through his fingers and drip onto the faded knees of his blue polyester suit.

"I was never happy with Bonnie," he confessed. "And she was never happy with me. Our families forced us to marry, and our marriage was miserable. I could barely stand to be in the same room with her, and the feeling was quite mutual. There's no other reason for what I did. It's not a valid reason, I know, but it's the truth. That makes what I did even more bitter."

"We've all done bitter things."

"As bitter as murder?" He looked to me. "It's not as if I coveted my neighbor's coat or stole a loaf of bread. I poisoned my wife and buried her in a shallow grave. Oh!" He gasped. "That's the first time I've ever spoken those words aloud! How wretched I am. My sin is severe."

"Whoever keeps the whole law yet stumbles at one point is guilty of breaking it all, Mr. Huxley. We all stumble. Doesn't that make us all equal offenders? I'm learning that I can't possibly judge you for what you've done when I have my own burden to bear, when we all fall short. I can't merely love only those whom I consider deserving of that love. I've lived that way far too long."

He pondered my words and slowly nodded.

"Your ma showed you these things? She raised you well, Ursula."

"She is still raising me well, Mr. Huxley."

"Hello, dear."

"Ma."

"Good things this week?"

"We're inundated with three feet of snow."

Ma laughed. "That's a good thing?"

"It's vile. I long for spring."

"I know you do, dear. Like water, your blood. It's always failed to keep you warm."

"I require blood as thick as chowder to keep me warm in this." I glanced out the window of the diner to see the dreaded precipitation steadily falling from the night sky.

"You've been shut in then? Unable to do many good things this week?"

"I've managed to do some," I said. "I took Grenada Silverdean a quiche and kept Ms. Finglo company. We played a card game of Ninetails."

"Oh! That dear Ms. Finglo! How is she getting on? Still speaking to her furniture?"

"The furniture was beginning to respond! Physician Tryce put a stop to that when he finally increased her medication. It only took him three years to help her, but it's done."

"Well, I'm certainly glad to hear that!"

"I did help Barton Huxley, Ma."

"Oh, Ursula," she paused. "I'm certainly glad to hear that

as well."

"I gave him Papa's work boots. I hope you do approve."

"Approve, Ursula?" I could hear the smile forming on her beautiful, glowing face. "I could not approve of anything more."

"I was unsure how you would feel. Papa's shoes were so special to—"

"They're special to Barton Huxley now, Ursula. Your papa has no need for those shoes. What good can they do setting by a door or hidden in a wardrobe?"

"I invited Mr. Huxley inside to take shelter from the blizzard. He drank tea and warmed his hands by the fire. We had a cathartic talk, Barton Huxley and I. He slept on my couch two evenings and disappeared this morning. There was a letter left on my bureau thanking me for my kindness— and thanking you."

"Thanking me?" Ma asked.

"He knows your words of wisdom convinced me to appreciate the good in sinners— to help all despite their past."

"I didn't convince you of any such thing, Ursula. You're responsible for healing the intolerance that resided in your heart."

"I would not say healed quite yet, Ma."

"Oden Barmouth continues to be a stumbling block in your healing, I assume?"

"He does." I nodded.

"That will change with time. You are travelling the good and noble path. You're marching in love, dear daughter. Continue on."

"Shiloh Pethlen."

"A name I have not heard in years," Ma responded.

"I went to see him, Ma. I went to the penitentiary and saw downtown's most notorious criminal."

"You saw him, Ursula? Why?"

"After our last conversation, his name would not leave me be. I knew the first step in healing any prejudice would be to help the one man everyone south of the Winnow despises. And Ma," I said, "I found Shiloh Pethlen to be quite refreshing."

"Dear?"

"He's quite a lovely man and quite repentant of his wickedness, as well. I sat in front of his cell, Ma, and spoke to this thin shell of a man who has spent the majority of his life in that dreary and dark hole, and I was at such peace. His words, his voice alone, gave me great peace– just like yours. I never would have considered visiting him if you had not given me insight in loving the unlovable. After all, you love me. Leaving you the way I did was unforgiveable and certainly unlovable."

"My dear, you are my child and nothing you do could stifle my adoration for you. And you must stop taking blame! You had to leave me. You did nothing wrong, Ursula! It was time for you to go," she insisted. "As for praising me, you oughtn't. I can only give you advice. I cannot love the unlovable for you, Ursula. You are responsible for your actions. You give me too much credit."

"And you give me too much, Ma."

"Shiloh Pethlen! Even I have never laid eyes upon the man."

"He said Oden Barmouth spent time in the cell near his. He said that Oden sobbed nightly for what he'd done to Papa."

Ma remained silent.

"That is supposed to sway me to feel pity for Oden Barmouth, innit, but I still do not. So, Ma, my intolerance has not fully healed."

"Love fully heals, Ursula, and you have an abundance of that. Let it continue to do its work. You've given shoes and shelter to a man who poisoned his wife. You've visited a murderer who hasn't seen a glimpse of the outside world in 40 years. The love within you is working diligently. It's healing diligently."

"I have so much other news," I said quietly and shielded my hand over my mouth and the phone receiver so no one could hear. "I visited Pype's home. He divulged that his brother-in-law is Tavish Dunbryll, Ma. Shaw Dunbryll's son! And he is sympathetic to southerners! There's chance his sister's husband is going to make peace when he becomes the heir! And I received word across the bridge that Mayor Dunbryll is ill. What if peace is imminent? Oh, Ma, I cannot imagine."

"Oh, Ursula." Ma exhaled in relief. "Oh, sweet, Ursula."

"Do you know the future, Ma? Do you see what will be? Do you know if we'll obtain peace in my lifetime?"

"These things I do not know," she answered.

"There's something else," I said. "I saw a woman over the bridge. She had fiery red hair and a little girl named Rupalia. I sketched her daughter and spoke with her briefly. She knew Grandmother. We must be related, Ma. I've never seen hair that hue since our journey to Wheatsand decades ago."

"Marigold," Ma answered almost in a whisper. "My sister, Marigold."

"You believe the woman is Marigold's daughter?"

"She must be. When you were an infant, I saw Marigold over the bridge one hot, humid day. She had a baby in her arms as well, not much older than you. That child had Mother's blazing hair. Marigold saw me across the way and rushed into a housewares store. I never saw her again. And Rupalia was my grandmother's name."

"I've often wondered if I passed relations on northern streets. I have searched faces and eavesdropped for names. Never, until now, have I realized that my blood is running through a

~ 89 ~

northerner's veins– a Wheatsand resident's veins. Maybe it's thin blood as mine."

"I loved my sister very much. Until I married your father, she loved me as well. We skipped rocks on Nils Lake and frolicked through the fields of cattails. We braided one another's hair and shared secrets. Marigold was my best friend, a dear gift from the Most High, and it hurt me greatly that she forfeited that love because I chose a southern man. Oh, I knew I'd never be allowed back to Wheatsand when I moved downtown with your father, but I expected my departure to be different. I expected my dear sister to cry and beg me to stay. I never assumed she'd stand before me with fists clenched and declare in anger that I was dead to her. I knew leaving my family would be difficult, but I expected to carry a bit of their love with me to the south side. I was unable to do so."

"You sacrificed greatly for love, Ma."

"Marigold and Mother sacrificed as well, I know, but it turned them rigid and cold."

"If I see her again, Ma, what should I do?"

"You'll do nothing, Ursula. Because of my choices, albeit choices I never regretted, your cousin will opt to have nothing to do with you. You treat her as any other Wheatsand resident– you treat her with kindness and love, but you treat her as a stranger."

"Pity, innit, Ma? Pity we are forced to live this way merely because of our geographic location. Pity we aren't accepted by family."

"If what you say is true and Mayor Dunbryll's heir concedes to bring peace to both sides of the Winnow, things might change. You may dine on holiday lamb in the great dining room in the shadow of Brannock Castle."

"Even if it is true and peace is pending, Ma, I still do not expect those who live in the north and in Wheatsand to accept southerners so willingly. Years of intolerance and prejudice will see to that."

"Negativity doesn't suit you."

"Yes. And Papa?"

"You know I can't."

"Yes, Ma."

"Go do good things, dear. I love you. Always."

"Always."

NINE

On Tuesday, I woke to the relentless sound of water dripping and an orange hue piercing through the drop cloth curtain in my bedroom. My dear friend, the sun, had returned to bring warmth to my bones and clear the sidewalks of sludge. I didn't realize I was smiling until I threw my long white legs over the side of the feather bed, stood and saw my reflection in the mirror beside the wardrobe.

I rested against the kitchen counter and sipped the blackcurrant tea, eager to dress and leave my apartment. I would skip data entry for the day and double up on the workload tomorrow. The blizzard had kept me trapped in the house for far too long. I relished in the opportunity to walk down the street and maintain dry boots.

The loosely-tied scarf bounced across my shoulder as I nearly skipped over the stagnant puddles on the sidewalks. The warmth of the sun radiated throughout my body. I could not remember the last time that magnificent, warm sphere had kissed my cheeks. I savored every toasty moment.

Barton Huxley seemed to be savoring it as well. When I dropped the coins into his mug, he looked up at me with bright eyes and a forehead tinted by the rays. "Thank you, Ursula," he spoke and nodded.

In fact, everyone I passed on the street seemed to have lifted spirits and lighter feet. We exchanged nods and smiles and pleasantries such as, "Beautiful day, innit?" while the delicious smell of Ms. Purvis' fresh bread topped with strawberry butter wafted on air that didn't seem as bitter and cruel as usual. Even the cats on 8th wagged their tails and purred with content.

I leaned against the familiar cracked column at the soup kitchen and noticed the usual sounds of grumbling and woe had been replaced with lighthearted laughter and cheery tones. What a magnificent thing that sun was– beaming through the gaps in the coliseum roof! It was nearly medicinal to the poor and destitute on the south side of the Winnow River.

Pype filled the cardboard bowls with the day's special, lentil soup, and Gunnar topped each helping with a sliver of cornbread. The homeless passed me while carrying their lunch back to the square. Their gloves were hidden away in their pockets, and their coats were unbuttoned, thanks to the free heater in the sky.

As he served the hungry, I could not help but notice Pype's haircut. It suited him. Shaggy locks no longer concealed his coffee-colored eyes and high cheekbones. He truly looked like a northerner– clean cut and well-groomed with a wide grin and the sun shining on his face.

"Ursula," he said when he stepped away from the serving table.

"I fancy your hair, Mr. Tyburn."

"Oh yes? Mrs. Percival did the job." He ran his hand across the top of his head. "It was getting entirely too long and unkempt. You know how I feel about unkempt."

"Certainly I do."

"Would you like a bowl today? There's plenty to go around. It's fairly tasty. Gunnar made the cornbread. He's a right good cook."

"No, thank you." I shook my head. "I was just stopping by to say hello. I had to get out of my apartment."

"This sun is glorious, innit?" He looked to the bright sky through the missing patch of roof. "Mighty long overdue."

"That it is. Did you fare well in the blizzard?"

"Yes." He shoved his hands into the pockets of his brown pants. "But I was unable to get down here to serve for two days."

"Bless these poor people. Where did they all go with so many feet of snow covering their beds? The wind chill was deadly. I'm surprised so many lived through it."

"Thirty-two of them came to my home. Another ten went to Gunnar's flat. Mr. Tackett on Valoria took a dozen or so. I only pray the others found shelter and aren't soon accounted for, blue and bloated, in the alleys or by the river."

"Thirty-two, Pype? My mercy!" I exclaimed. "Where'd you put them all?"

"Wherever I could."

"And what kind of toll did that take on your sanity? I assume thirty-two vagrants do not keep their coats hanging on the hall tree and their dishes in the sink."

Pype laughed. "I did the best I could to overlook it. I panicked a bit, yes, but I'm quite proud that I didn't resort to drinking troughs of grain alcohol while they were my guests! Not that I minded their company, no. They were all quite interesting people with heart-wrenching stories and terribly grateful for a roof over their heads. The spilled coffee on the couch and the mud on the rug proved to be the only challenges."

I smiled. "I do not know your mother, Pype, but I know she must be a wise woman. You do, indeed, have a servant's heart."

He grinned and blushed. "You want to take a walk, Ursula? I'm through here for a little while, and it's quite a perfect day for it."

"I think," I answered and nodded, "that's a grand idea."

Pype and I crossed the east side of Mabyn Square and emerged onto Valoria Bend. The noonday sun blanketed us with warmth as we walked the curvy street.

"My sister's house is there." I pointed to the green wooden one-level in the turn. The front porch swing with chipped white paint swayed in the wind and reflected on the mud puddles that consumed the front yard.

"Not a bad place," Pype said.

"There's plenty of bad there."

"Oh." Pype glanced over at me.

"Lolly and her beau, Thad, aren't the most pleasant couple. There is plenty of abuse behind that burgundy door. Beatings, crying and infidelity— it all lives there."

"I'm quite sorry to hear that, Ursula."

"Well." I shrugged. "Nothing I can do about it, yeah? I have cautioned my sister time and time again, but you simply cannot help those who are not willing to help themselves."

We rounded the bend and soon my sister's home was no longer in sight. I tilted my face to the sun and welcomed the heat coloring my cheeks.

"Lovely, innit?" Pype asked.

"The north can take so many things from us, but they cannot take this, can they?"

"No they cannot." Pype smiled.

"I crossed over the bridge last week." I tilted my head back down. "There's word that the mayor has taken ill."

"Is there?" Pype asked as we entered the thick tree line of Hannelore Park.

"I overheard a woman in the registry line saying she'd heard at the apothecary that ole Dunbryll is coming to an end. I could not help but think what you'd said about his son, Tavish."

"My sister has not sent word that Dunbryll is ill. Surely she would have let me know in one of her letters hidden behind the whitewashed brick."

"Speculation then, innit?"

"Northerners have speculated about Dunbryll's death for years." Pype kicked a pine cone. "He's quite advanced in age, and they all know his passing is forthcoming. I assume they are confused by what Tavish's rule would bring. They recognize he's not quite the same as his father."

"How is that so? He's made it apparent that he's sympathetic to the south?"

"No, certainly not," Pype said, "but he just does not seem like the sort to rule with the same iron fist they are accustomed to. Anyone who's ever been around Tavish more than two minutes knows he's somewhat of a sweetheart. He's a soft man, kind and caring. He certainly isn't the type of mayor to behead penniless southern widows for swiping mittens from a boutique. It's evident."

"If Shaw Dunbryll was to cross over in the near future and your brother-in-law was to overturn the decree and consider us equals again, there would be uprisings wouldn't there? Those in the mayor's cabinet would never stand for it would they? They wouldn't merely welcome us back over the bridge with open arms and share their wealth with us. Galvan Montagne and Chester Bramblewood would not be given positions at the palladium mine. Things would never–"

"Negativity doesn't suit you, Ursula," Pype interrupted me.

"That's what Ma says," I mumbled.

"I have no doubt there would be obstacles, but I also know that the mayor has the final say. There is no democracy north of the Winnow– only dictatorship. If Tavish declares that we are to be equals, then we just are. There is no overturning the mayor's stance."

"Would any of them agree, though? Would any be content with the decision?"

"Some would, I suspect— the older ones who remember life before the Cronin Civil War. They'll remember the peace between both banks of the river and how things were once fair and balanced. Dunbryll was the one who incited division when he was elected 57 years ago. Do you even know how that began? Do they teach that in southern elementary?" Pype looked to me.

"Not officially, no. We're only taught from the books that northern professors have written. We all know the teaching materials aren't accurate because we've heard stories of the past from our elders who lived through it, but how the war actually began isn't common knowledge among the younger generation," I said.

"I know for certain."

"Tell me, Pype," I requested as the dense woods shielded my back from the sun.

"Dunbryll was born in Wheatsand 80 years ago, the grandson of King Brannock. He grew up in the castle at the epicenter of the city, wanting for nothing. He attended the best schools and vacationed often by the Welshlynn Sea. On a trip to the north side of the Winnow when he was 20 or so, he fell in love with a young maiden who was the daughter of a palladium broker. They courted for quite some time, and Dunbryll was content to take her to Wheatsand to live in Brannock Castle with his family. However, she was caught courting another— a lowly southern man."

"Dunbryll was heartbroken by the betrayal? And then what?"

"He was." Pype took my hand and helped me climb over a fallen tree trunk. "He vowed then that he'd somehow make the southern people suffer. He looked down on them, the mere working class, and desired that they would no longer be allowed to cross the bridge and take sophisticated northern women."

"My mother grew up to do that very thing– to fall in love with a southern man and leave her life in Wheatsand behind."

"She did, did she?"

"Oh yes," I answered. "And she never regretted it for a moment."

"Well, it came to be that the former mayor of the north, Durcell Pendland, fell ill and had no heir to take his place as mayor. Shaw Dunbryll volunteered, and it is assumed that he paid off Pendland's cabinet with a tidy sum to support his reign. Only months after he'd been in office, he placed a fear of southerners into everyone on the north side. He labeled them as beggars and thieves and murderers. He painted the south as a dreadful place. He waged war on that very fear, and Wheatsand rallied behind him. Thus, the Cronin Civil War began. And I do believe it's no coincidence that his former lover and her southern beau, Boyle Huxley, were both killed in the first battle. They left an infant boy orphaned."

"Huxley! The baby must've been Barton. You know the man on the corner of 9th and Gwinnett?"

"The old chap with the cardboard sign and pink scarf?"

"Barton Huxley," I whispered.

"Must be," Pype said. "The hatred and division between the banks of the Winnow is merely based on one man's heartbreak. The schoolbooks will lead you to believe that southerners marched over the Winnow at the order of General Simeon Cronin and demanded control of the palladium mine, but that simply is not true. I've heard these words straight from Shaw Dunbryll's mouth while he dined on lamb and laughed patronizingly."

"We've always been painted as the ones to incite the war."

"Folly, Ursula. It's all folly."

"And Tavish Dunbryll knows that such hatred and unfairness is all to blame on his father's heartache? It's to blame on the choice made by Barton Huxley's mother?"

"Tavish knows the intricacies. I believe he would bring peace to both sides. Mabyn State would be united once again under his rule. No north or south. We'd be one again, the way Dessick Mabyn intended 200 years ago."

"It would be a dream, Pype."

"The thing I fear would be Tavish's assassination. A member of the cabinet or Shaw's youngest son, Shacklee, would be adamantly against a new treaty for peace. Shacklee is a wretched man with a heart of hatred that he inherited from his father. He'd be the next in line if Tavish was gone. A state under the rule of Shacklee Dunbryll would be terrifying– more terrifying than anything we've ever known. He'd forbid us to ever visit the north. He'd shut down every business on the south side. He'd pillage crops. We'd starve."

"I cannot imagine–" Pype and I stopped quickly and silenced the echo of the dead leaves crunching beneath our feet.

Ahead of us only 30 yards or so was a family of four. Father, mother, two small girls with eyes open, cracked white skin and lips the color of blueberries. They sat on the ground, leaned against a massive Runyon trunk, frozen arms linking them together. Dead.

TEN

I sprinted into town and alerted the squad while Pype stayed behind with the family claimed by the blizzard. Soon half a dozen uniformed men followed me into the woods thawed by the day's sun. They carefully carried each member out of Hannelore Park on a canvas gurney. The father was lugged out last, melting snow still dripping from his bushy beard, and Pype and I were left alone in the woods.

I didn't know what to say and neither did Pype. We just stood there motionless for several minutes. When the silence became deafening, we walked across the crisp leaves toward the Winnow River. Tears threatened to escape my eyes and sorrow threatened to consume me, but I stifled those emotions and tried to focus on the cheerfulness found in the sun.

"You knew them?" I could bear the silence no longer.

"Yes," Pype replied somberly. "The youngest girl, Bernadette, was quite partial to the corn and coconut. She wanted to live on an island where coconuts grow in abundance. I once told her about the productive tree line along the Welshlynn Sea. Her face simply glowed when she imagined that stunning place."

"Pype." I reached over and lightly touched his arm. "You could not save them all."

"I looked for them when I invited everyone to my home the first night that the snow fell. I really did look for them. I inquired about them. I do not know what possessed them to go into the woods. Maybe they thought they would be sheltered by the Runyon trees."

"They're fortunate now, though, aren't they,? No more seeking shelter or food. They've crossed over, Pype. There are worse things."

He glanced at me. "You must have lost someone dear to

you, Ursula. Only those who truly grieve find great comfort in what lies on the other side."

"I have," I said as we exited the woods and walked along the banks of the river, the sun once again beaming upon us. "My father died when I was quite young– only three. The man who killed him lives right up this way." I pointed ahead.

"Was there a motive for your father's murder?" Pype asked softly.

"No." I shook my head. "Papa tried to stop a man from robbing the pawn shop and was shot in the process. His killer, Oden Barmouth, spent many years at the penitentiary, but he's out now. He lives there."

Pype followed my finger to the derelict shack on the muddy bank of the Winnow River. The scent of drying muck engulfed us, and the bright sun gleaming on the tin roof reflected into our eyes. We didn't slow, and I didn't pay close enough attention to see if Oden Barmouth was sitting inside and staring at nothing.

"My mother keeps pressing me to forgive him, but I'm not yet ready. I'd be lying if I said I even want to forgive him. Somehow I thrive on the hatred I feel for the man who killed my father. Papa was a good man– honest and decent. He loved me and my mother more than anything in this wretched place. My sister never even knew him. He died too soon."

"But he's one of the fortunate ones now, isn't he? He's crossed over, Ursula, with no burden of this world's worries. You believe that?"

"That's the only thing that gives me peace."

"If your ma has forgiven the man who made her a widow then certainly you must try. The love for a father is strong indeed, but no stronger than the love for a husband."

"My mother is a better woman than me. She's noble and

gentle and good and kind."

"And you aren't?" Pype asked.

"She has the ability to love unconditionally."

"And you don't?"

"I'm working on it," I said.

As the glorious sun began to set and the dreaded chill found its way back into the winter air, Pype and I strolled through town toward Mabyn Square. We tried to forget the unfortunate family that we'd discovered in the woods and instead talked about Pype's childhood and his trips to the Welshlynn Sea. He'd witnessed the mysterious turtles nesting and rescued a dolphin from a fisherman's net on his last vacation there. He told me about his fine education and laughed at the navy blazer and shorts, sweater vest, striped tie, wool socks and shiny oxfords that he wore daily. He described the day he purchased Aiko from a breeder in Wheatsand and the dog's remarkable ability to retrieve downed waterfowl. He spoke with a hint of sadness at days gone by, yet he also spoke with hope that more happy memories were to be made.

"What about your ma, Ursula. Have we passed her home? I'd love to meet her. She sounds like a very delightful woman, indeed, with her nobleness, kindness and ability to love unconditionally."

I ignored Pype's remark because my eyes were fixated on Thaddeus Jessop stumbling out of the ale house on 5th Street. He wiped his mouth with the back of his arm, hiccupped and steadied himself on his feet. He wasn't in his squad uniform but instead dressed head-to-toe in black. Even his buzzed hair was covered in a black flat cap.

"Who is it?" Pype followed my stare.

"Thad," I replied. "He's been drinking. Lolly will be in for it this evening."

Thad stopped on the cobblestone street and leaned his body against the front of the deserted building that once served as Blaylock's Eatery. He struck a match and attempted to light the cigarette hanging from his lips, but the brisk wind extinguished the flame. He tossed the useless match to the ground and attempted it again with no success. Again, he tried to light the rolled tobacco, but by this try, Pype and I had reached him. Pype dug into his pocket, pulled out his own book of matches, struck one along the matchbook and reached over to light Thad's cigarette.

"Oh!" He startled at Pype before drawing on the cigarette with pursed lips. "Thanks, old chap."

"Hello, Thad," I said.

"Oh how lovely," he smirked at me before looking to Pype. "What are you doing hanging around such rubbish as this, old chap?"

"Rubbish? That's no way to speak of your sister-in-law, now is it?" Pype asked.

"But she's rubbish, indeed," Thad sneered. "This one is always sticking her nose in other's affairs. Isn't that right, Unfortunate Ursula Underwood?"

"How do you know me by that name?" I questioned. "Lolly would never utter it. She knows the weight it bears."

"Possibly I just came up with it right this minute. It's not quite difficult to decipher! Your name is Ursula Underwood and you're quite the unfortunate one, aren't you? A lonely, fatherless spinster who is responsible for her own poor mother's—"

"That'll be enough," Pype interrupted, "old chap."

Thad looked at Pype gruffly for a moment before laughing arrogantly. "You're her beau then? You are the beau of Ursula Underwood?" He laughed again.

~ 104 ~

"I'm a friend."

"Oh!" Thad shrugged and inhaled smoke. "Of course you are. What was I thinking? As if someone would want plain Ursula in *that* way. Bet you'd like to sew her mouth shut so you wouldn't have to hear her bloody nagging all the time, right? Maybe get her drunk so she'll loosen up a bit and not be such a stick in the mud, too, eh?" Thad laughed heartily.

I looked to the ground, ashamed by the truth that Thaddeus had spoken of me. I was plain. I did nag my sister relentlessly. I had always been told to loosen up. Thad knew my truth.

"And another thing," his tone turned angry as he pointed his black gloved finger in my face, "the next time you beg your sister to leave me and move in with you, I'll teach you! Lolly is mine. She always has been, and she always will be. You're wasting your–" In midsentence, Pype reared back his fist and hit Thad square in the jaw, knocking the cigarette from the corner of his mouth and jerking him into the brick building behind him where he slid to the cobblestone.

"Pype!" I exclaimed.

Pype shook his hand, massaged his fist and muttered through clenched teeth.

"Are you okay?" I reached for his throbbing knuckles.

"I'm fine," he said. "I'm loads better than him anyway, aren't I?" He nodded to Thad knocked out cold on the sidewalk. "Should we wake him? Move him indoors? He's quite soiled lying there in that murky puddle, but I really don't want to dirty my shirt."

"I've a good mind to kick him square in the chin. Twice," I said. "Let's just leave him and go."

"Pleasant chap, isn't he?" Pype asked as we scurried away.

"That wasn't quite wise," I said. "He'll be looking for you

now. He works with the squad. He'll prey on every opportunity to damage you. He'll look for any reason to shut down the soup kitchen, as well. It wasn't wise, Pype."

"He wasn't wise, what spewing that garbage. I was not going to let him insult you in that way. He deserved my measly hit and loads more."

"Your hand?" I took it into mine and examined it by the porch lights now illuminating on Gwinnett. "Is it broken?"

"Eh, it's fine. It's barely throbbing now. I can still ladle soup just fine."

"It just wasn't wise," I repeated.

"The name he called you. Unfortunate? What weight does that bear?"

"It's nothing." I shook my head.

"It's something."

I gave a lengthy sigh before reluctantly speaking, "A girl I went to school with called me by that name. She harassed me for years and found great pleasure in pointing out how unfortunate I was– I am."

"You believe you're unfortunate, Ursula?" Pype looked over to me as I shrugged. "Do you know the meaning of the word?"

"Yes." I looked at him, slightly offended at his remark.

"Your father being murdered wasn't of good fortune, I agree, but what else do you have to categorize you as such? Did you grow up dirt poor? Have you hungered many days of your life? Been without a roof over your head? Abandoned by your parents?"

"No." I shook my head.

"Well, that's right fortunate, innit? It sounds to me that the girl who bullied you in school didn't know the proper meaning of the word. It sounds to me that she was an ignorant fool."

"Thad is correct, though. I do nag. I'm boring. I'm plain. Those are all right unfortunate character traits."

"He's a fool as well," Pype said. "You nag whom? Your sister? If cautioning someone because you love them is nagging, then by all means, I'd declare nagging a virtue."

"But I-" I began.

"And plain?" Pype laughed. "Who would dare prefer flashy clothes and dyed hair over natural beauty? If natural beauty is considered plain, then by all means, I'd declare plain a virtue as well."

I felt my pale cheeks blush at Pype's words.

"And we might as well address your claim that your company is not enjoyable. I've found more joy today in your presence than I have in quite some time, Ursula. Even despite the harrowing discovery in the woods, you've lightened my mood today. You're far from drab."

"Why do you tell me these things?" I asked as we crossed the charred street of Bally's Way.

"You don't even know it, but you are all of the adjectives that you've used to describe your ma— a woman you clearly idolize. You're noble and kind and I know you have the ability to love unconditionally."

We stopped at the edge of Mabyn Square now brightened with small fires blazing beneath the tarp and inside the tin garbage cans. I looked up at Pype Tyburn and knew exactly what good thing he required. I knew why Ma had pressed me to make his acquaintance. Pype Tyburn wasn't merely looking for a friend. He was looking for love.

I'd only loved one— Prentice Fawkes. And, of course, that hadn't fared well. I had drawn his name in my composition book and fantasized about our wedding at the dainty chapel on Persephone. I'd envisioned our children– blonde, chunky babies that resembled the one who rested on Staley's hip while she hung clothes on the line. I was content that I'd spend forever gazing into Prentice Fawkes' sparkling blue eyes and running my fingers through his sandy hair. When we met at the diner one beautiful spring weekend over 15 years ago, I thought my pounding heart was going to leap out of my chest. And I spent night after night sobbing on my pillow after I learned that he had only used me to invoke jealousy. Why he picked me, I didn't know, and I even clung to some sort of hope that he secretly pined for me– that's why he chose me to use. And once I stopped crying myself to sleep night after night, I swore I'd never put myself through such heartache again. I'd never cry over another. I'd never allow my heart to palpitate at the very sight of another.

But at that moment, as I gazed up at Pype Tyburn's rugged face glowing in the moonlight, my heart palpitated. It fluttered. It leapt.

"I must go." I gulped. "Thank you for a lovely day, Pype."

"I'll call on you soon, Ursula?"

I nodded, turned and quickly walked back to Downforge Alley.

ELEVEN

"Mr. Huxley?" I knelt down to him and whispered.

Barton shifted beneath the newsprint, slowly turned his head toward me and opened his eyes.

"Oh, Ursula!" He quickly sat upright.

"Mr. Huxley, I'm sorry to wake you, but I must speak to you about something," I said and squatted down next to him on the cold pavement.

"What is it? Is everything quite alright?" He batted his eyes and yawned.

"Do you know much of your parents?"

He shook his head, confused. "My parents died in the war when I was an infant. I was taken in by our neighbors, Mr. and Mrs. Balthar."

"They didn't tell you why your parents died?"

"They died because they were southerners, Ursula. They died for the same reason hundreds of others did."

"I learned some information today concerning them, Mr. Huxley. All afternoon I've wrestled with whether or not to tell you the specifics, but I believe you should know."

"*My* parents? You're sure?"

"Boyle Huxley?"

"Yes." Barton nodded. "Boyle and Herriot Huxley were my father and mother."

"Before they were married, your mother courted Shaw Dunbryll."

"She didn't." He shook his head and shifted his back against the old hardware store. "That's impossible. She'd always lived south of the Winnow with my father. She wasn't associated with the upper-class."

"She was the daughter of a palladium broker, Mr. Huxley.

She was raised on the affluent northern side. Shaw Dunbryll loved your mother and had intentions to take her to Wheatsand with him, but she fell for another. She fell for your father."

He sat silent and motionless.

"Shaw Dunbryll allowed his broken heart to turn him bitter and cruel. He was terribly scorned and vowed to rule the north and banish southerners from ever living across the river again. He vowed never to let another southern man claim a northern woman."

"This is farfetched," he said and shook his head in disbelief, "but if what you are saying is true, you are giving me another burden to bear, Ursula. You are telling me that my mother was responsible for the Cronin Civil War."

"I feared you would interpret it that way, and that is why I was conflicted in sharing this with you, Mr. Huxley," I answered, "but don't you see how proud you should be?"

"Proud?" he asked, confused. "Proud that my mother's decision to marry my father resulted in the deaths of hundreds and the atrocious way that we are forced to live? It's my mother's fault that people starve and are beaten— that we are only allowed across the bridge a few times a month."

"No," I said. "Your mother was an incredibly courageous woman. Like my mother, she chose to marry the man that she loved despite the ominous consequences. She did not die in vain, Mr. Huxley. She was courageous enough to die for love. That same strength and courage flows through your veins."

"I cannot see it that way, Ursula. It is just another burden to bear."

"It is not, Mr. Huxley. It was not your mother's fault that Shaw Dunbryll is the epitome of evil. It is not your burden to bear." I stood from the cold pavement.

"We see things differently," he replied.

"Perhaps we do, Mr. Huxley, but I certainly hope you'll consider the way I interpret it. There's no burden in it at all– only pride."

My mind raced as I restlessly tossed in my bed. The bedroom was comfortably dark and quiet with the exception of the brass blades of the oscillating fan slicing through the night air, yet sleep eluded me.

The image of Pype Tyburn was engrained in my mind– his confident stride, the way he ran his fingers through his fresh haircut and then shoved his hands into the pockets of his meticulously clean apron. I repeatedly replayed his complimentary words and the declaration of my natural beauty and pleasurable company. His eyes, the color of coffee with a dash of cream, were visible every time I closed my own. Pype Tyburn had overtaken my mind the same way Prentice Fawkes had so many years ago. And I did not like it at all.

I turned to my left side and huffed in aggravation. Garfunkel, too, seemed bothered with my tossing as he purred and made an impatient circle at my feet before finally resting on his stomach.

"I do not want to think of this man, *or any man*, Garfunkel," I spoke into the night. "I'm agitated with Ma, silly cat. I've made it abundantly clear to her over the years that I have no desire to long for a man and risk being heartbroken and devastated again. Surely she knew that connecting me with Pype would lead to these very feelings that are keeping us both awake tonight. I'll be sure to bring it up to her on Sunday." Garfunkel responded by irritably turning in another circle.

It was evident that Pype was a kind and caring man. He selflessly served others each day and left a pleasant northern life behind to live in a khaki loft that overlooked a dreary southern penitentiary. I did find these attributes attractive, but again, I was vehemently opposed to sharing my life with anyone no matter how equally yoked we seemed to be. I was content living alone and entering data and helping those in need and staring out a window with a purring companion. I certainly did not desire a man to interrupt my lifestyle.

I opted to steer my mind in a different direction. I thought of Barton Huxley and the new information that swam in his own head and probably kept him awake on the corner of 9th and Gwinnett. I worried that I had done wrong by revealing the truth concerning his parents, although I fervently believed that his mother's decision was far from dishonorable. I truly yearned that he would eventually see it the same way.

Then I focused on Finley and his likely need for more licorice root. Mora Sloane then floated into my thoughts, and I mulled over options to help her although I desperately did not want to do so. Oden Barmouth drifted in, as well, but I was certainly not yet ready to do any good thing for him.

Lolly appeared next, her face covered with shame and hurt and tears, as I often saw her, followed by a vision of that despicable Thad. And then I was reminded of Pype hammering Thaddeus in the nose and cursing at the pain. My mind had been led right back to Pype Tyburn and those dark eyes and wide smile—

"No, Garfunkel! I refuse to think about him!" I shouted at the sleeping cat.

I turned to my right side, placed the pillow over my face and then squeezed my eyes closed as tightly as possible. I only removed the feathery cushion when suffocation set in. When I pulled it from my nose, the sound of angry voices echoed outside my bedroom window.

I threw my feet onto the cold parquet floor and scurried over to the glass to see a small group of men huddled beneath the streetlamp across from my building. Galvan and Chester stood on the right side of the cluster. Chester had his fists raised in defense.

I quietly lifted the heavy paned window and listened to their voices resounding on the sharp, icy air.

"If you attempt to take a single coin, it will be the last thing you ever attempt!" Chester shouted crossly.

The three men standing across from Galvan and Chester were obviously northerners. From the dim light of the lamp, I could see their perfectly pressed slacks and starched shirt tails hanging beneath their leather coats.

I dashed away from the window and into the living room, a sleepy and irritated Garfunkel following. I hurriedly buttoned my wool coat over my nightgown, tightened the sash and put my socked feet into the black boots next to my door. As I scurried down the stairway, I had no idea what my intentions were. Why I was running directly to an altercation between three northerners and my friends was beyond me. I knew I could be of no service, but I hurried toward them anyway.

"Chester?" I panted warm puffs of air.

"Ursula, go back inside!" he shouted at me.

"You've no business here," Galvan chimed.

"Are you in trouble?" I tightly folded my arms in hopes to produce a little warmth.

"Well, who have we here, Chester? Is this your guardian?" One of the northern men laughed beneath a dark fedora.

"Ursula, this is none of your affair. Go home," Chester demanded.

"Ursula?" the man in the fedora asked. "I knew an Ursula

once. Mighty fine woman she was. Not nearly as plain as you, of course." He clicked his tongue and gave a sly grin.

"I prefer them plain," another northern man with a pencil-thin mustache said. "You know exactly what you are getting. Eye pencil and rouge and yellow hair dye are merely deceptions."

"Ursula." Galvan shook his head and gritted his teeth. "Stubborn Ursula."

"Have you come looking for a fight, Ursula?" Fedora asked.

"I've come to see what issue you have with my friends. Coins, I suppose?"

"I don't believe this is your affair now is it?" the third northerner spoke. He was a nervous man with tortoiseshell glasses and a white beard.

"Do you know my friends personally or have you ventured across the Nairn Bridge simply looking for fun? You're here to get your kicks and push around a few southerners and make a little loot in the process. That's right, innit?" I asked.

The three northern men exchanged glances before laughing.

"You've some nerve, Ursula. Feisty, aren't you?" Fedora stepped closer to me. "You're like some sort of hero taking cover in the night and coming to the rescue of your pitiable and pathetic people. Are you supernatural, Ursula? Like the champions in the books? Are lightning bolts going to fly from your fingers and singe us all? Is that how you're going to save the day?"

"That's absurd," I answered. "If I were allowed any supernatural power, it would be the power of invisibility. Then I would cross the bridge any time that I liked."

"Let me tell you what is going to happen here, Ursula." He took another step, his garlic-scented breath drifting to my face. "We are going to take your friends' coins, no matter how few they are and no matter what brute force we have to execute to obtain those coins. Not because we know them personally or because we have a great need for coins, but because we simply can. Once we are done with them, we're going to see fit what to do with you. I have no need for you, but it seems Garrick likes them plain." He nodded to his friend with the thin mustache. "I believe he has a birthday coming up, as well. Don't you, Garrick?"

"I do." Garrick smiled wickedly.

"What wonderful luck, Ursula! You'll serve a purpose here tonight after all! Not in the way that you'd hoped, by saving these pathetic fools that you call friends, but as a present for Garrick." He snickered and rubbed his hands together.

"I'd rather die," I barked through clenched teeth.

"Well, we can arrange that as well." He winked at me and turned back to Galvan and Chester. "Give us what coins you have along with what measly possessions are hidden in your pockets. Do this willingly and we will see that your guardian, Ursula, here is put out of her misery fairly quickly."

Galvan and Chester both looked at me, scared and ashamed, as they dug around in their pockets. Garrick stepped to me and tightly gripped the top of my arm.

"Don't do it. Don't give them a thing!" I shook my head. "I'm not afraid of them."

"You aren't?" Fedora asked. "Well, we'll make sure to change that very soon."

"Sir, what lot in life has caused your cruelty? Judging by that dapper hat and your supple leather coat, you've not suffered too greatly. What is the cause of your hatred? Did your parents fail to offer enough love? Have you been scorned by a woman? Or are you simply thriving on the revulsion that has been rooted in you by the declarations of Mayor Dunbryll? Tell me. I'd like to understand," I said as Garrick's grip tightened.

Fedora looked at me in surprise for a moment before giving his familiar malicious grin.

"You're quite the piece of work," he said. "Garrick, you may have to share your present. I don't believe she's quite as plain as I had originally suspected!"

"Do you feel repentance for these things that you do? Is there any moral dilemma brewing within you when you rob southerners and threaten women? Is there any light left within or are you dark through and through?"

"I've had enough–" he began.

"Ursula, stifle," Chester said.

"I believe I see a sliver of light behind those cold green eyes. There may be hope for you yet. As long as there is light within, you can grow. You can even find forgiveness if you truly repent for these sins that you commit. You're worthy of it. No one has ever told you that you're worthy, have they? That is why you do these things that you do?"

"Ursula," Chester pleaded.

I glanced at my southern friends with fear in their eyes and didn't even see the hit coming. I limply fell from Garrick's grip and felt my head strike the pavement before everything went dark.

When I woke, my face was numb, my right eyelid refused to open, and my head throbbed. My throat was incredibly parched, and sticky sweat dampened my chest. I slowly looked left and right with my one opened eye and realized that I was resting on my orange sofa in front of the roaring fire with dried blood covering my flannel nightgown.

My apartment was silent, but I worried that the northern men were near. I turned my stiff neck upward and saw Garfunkel resting in the windowsill. Dawn's light served as his background.

I attempted to slowly and carefully rise from the couch as

pain radiated from my stiff lower back up to my shoulders. The bloody scratches on my knuckles stung, and my legs felt terribly weak. I didn't remember anything past the first blow to the ground, and it was probably best that I didn't.

After a few deep breaths, I ignored the pain surging through my body and rose from the couch. I believed my apartment was empty until I heard the sound of raspy snoring coming from my bedroom. My heart leapt in my chest as I crept to the kitchen and retrieved a knife from the earthenware jar next to the stove. I glanced at the silly cat that was unaware of the dire situation and tip-toed toward my bedroom.

As my heart pounded, I turned the corner and finally saw the sleeping man in my bed. The face on my pillow belonged to Barton Huxley. His navy polyester coat was draped across the end of the bed near his bare feet that protruded from the mint green blanket.

"Mr. Huxley?" I nearly shouted while lowering the knife.

"Oh!" He snorted and jerked awake. "Ursula, are you quite alright?"

"I do not know, Mr. Huxley. Am I? Why are you in my bed?"

"Oh!" He threw his legs over the side. "Galvan, Chester and I saw fit to put you on the couch by the fire. We wanted you to be warm. I'm sorry I rested here." He stood. "I haven't had the pleasure of a bed in so long. I just wanted to sit on it for a moment until you woke, but I must have fallen asleep. That is a great level of disrespect, Ursula. I'm truly—"

"Enough," I said and turned back toward the living room. "What happened? Are Galvan and Chester quite alright? Where are the northerners?"

"We are fine." He followed me into the living room while putting his suit coat back on. "Sit down. I will fix you some tea. Blackcurrant?"

"Yes, please." I slowly lowered my aching body onto the couch.

"I saw the altercation occurring," he said and filled my kettle with brown water from the tap. "The sound of Chester's gruff voice prompted me to leave my corner and investigate. I was so scared when I heard your voice in the midst of it, as well. I waited behind your apartment."

"You saw the man in the fedora hit me then?"

"I did." He sat on the opposite end of the couch. "That's when I sprinted from the cover of the building. Galvan, Chester and I were able to take on all three. And then we brought you up here to warm by the fire. You were bleeding quite profusely from your injuries."

"Blood like water," I mumbled.

"I applied ointment to the gashes on your head and knuckles," he continued. "I found it in your bathroom cabinet. I hope you don't mind that I rummaged through your things trying to find medicine."

"Surely not, Mr. Huxley," I said. "I thank you."

"As soon as you dropped to the ground, the one with the fedora began kicking you. Chester dove on top of him. I took the one with the mustache, and Galvan handled the white-bearded one quite well."

"What became of them? Are they still lying on the street? Did they go back over the bridge?" I nodded to the window.

Barton immediately stood from the couch and shuffled his bare feet back to the kitchen. "Do you prefer your tea with sweetener?"

"Mr. Huxley, what happened to the northerners?" I twisted on the couch to face him. "Do tell me."

"They won't be hurting southerners anymore, Ursula. That's all you should know."

I gasped. "You killed them then? That's it, innit?"

Barton remained silent and watched the steaming kettle.

"Tell me, Mr. Huxley. That's it, innit? They are dead?"

"You shouldn't know such things, Ursula."

"Well, that answers my question." I turned back and stared

at the flame dancing on the logs in the fireplace.

"Everyone is quite better off for it," Barton mumbled.

"Where are they now? Where are their bodies?"

"More matters you oughtn't to know."

"In the woods, Mr. Huxley? Perhaps buried near your wife?"

In the window behind Garfunkel, I saw Mr. Huxley's reflection from the kitchen. He stared at the back of my head for a moment and remained expressionless before pouring the boiling water over the tea.

"Galvan and Chester handled it," he finally answered and brought me the silver cup.

"I don't fancy this a bit, Mr. Huxley. There is enough death and dying at the hands of northerners. Now we are no better than them. Those men deserved the chance of repentance! They deserved forgiveness," I said as he sat next to me on the sofa.

"Ursula." He leaned his elbows onto his bony polyester knees. "What your mother has taught you is quite moral. I don't disagree. She's taught you that love covers all. But I believe you have become clouded. You are disillusioned to trust that *all* people deserve forgiveness."

"Don't they, Mr. Huxley?"

"No." He shook his head in firm disagreement. "Some do, Ursula. You've taught me that those who truly repent do deserve forgiveness. But what does it mean to repent? Not merely to feel sincere remorse about one's wrongdoing but to cease doing it! Those men continually did vile things like this. See, I've seen them before. They've taken from me. They've harmed other southern women. They venture across the bridge every few seasons to wreak havoc merely for entertainment. That's simply evil, Ursula. Possibly they felt remorse for what they did, but they kept on doing it. That isn't true repentance."

"You are repentant for murdering your wife, aren't you, Mr. Huxley? But look what you've done this evening. You've killed yet again. You've made the same mistake again."

His eyes shifted to the floor. "I don't believe putting a stop to evil is a mistake."

I looked down at the steaming cup of tea and ran my scratched hand around the ceramic rim. "I see your point, Mr. Huxley. I truly do, but isn't there a possibility that those men would have eventually changed?"

"They were given many years to repent. And I believe some truly are evil to the core and are destined to harm anyone in their path until they spend eternity in fire. I thought I was that kind of evil until you came to me and shared the wisdom learned from your mother. And now I see the difference. I would never harm or kill an innocent again– an innocent as my Bonnie. I've felt sincere regret for that and will never do it again as long as I live. That is repentance. That is what, I'm finally learning, does deem forgiveness. But you have to know that some are just evil through and through, Ursula. You cannot help them all."

"Well that suits my campaign for not assisting Oden Barmouth. I'm certain he is truly evil."

"You're not certain about Oden Barmouth. I'm not certain about him either. But I am certain about these three northern men buried in the woods tonight. They'll never harm anyone again. And they surely would have."

"Well." I huffed. "I suppose there's a balance, innit, Mr. Huxley?"

"Yes, and I believe your ma would agree."

"I will be sure to ask her. In fact, I've many things to ask her." I scowled at the pain.

TWELVE

As I walked to the soup kitchen on Saturday morning, I slowed to examine my bruised face in Ms. Purvis' storefront window. I had attempted to conceal the marks with powder, but they were still evident. In four days, the abrasions had changed from blue to an unsightly shade that resembled pea soup.

I avoided eye contact with everyone I met on the street and crossed to the opposite sidewalk before I passed Staley Fawkes retrieving her child's clean clothes from the line on her porch. I certainly did not want her to notice my face and have a reason to relish in my misfortune.

Mr. Gunnar stood alone behind the long, narrow table and served slivers of breakfast bread to the hungry. It was highly unusual that Pype wasn't supervising. He rarely left a skittish Mr. Gunnar to work alone during the rush. I began to worry that Pype had fallen ill or worse— he had met Thad's retaliation.

Mr. Gunnar carefully placed a slice of toast topped with laver into a fuchsia-gloved hand protruding from a gray fleece coat. I followed the arm up to a face partially concealed by an oversized knit hat and black earmuffs. Still, I knew without doubt that the one receiving the bread was Mora Sloane.

She took her breakfast and quickly exited the back of the coliseum. Passing Mr. Gunnar and the dwindling line of hungry southerners, I followed her. I watched Mora avoid Valoria and enter a thin row of pines. She found a seat on a stump surrounded by prickly cones.

Remaining standoffish, I observed Mora Sloane rapidly shove chunks of toast into her mouth. She occasionally glanced from side to side as if she were nervous that she was being watched. I knew I should walk back inside the coliseum and leave my schoolyard nemesis to devour her food, but of course I rarely took my own advice.

Tucking my hands deep inside the lined pockets of my wool coat, I entered the trees. The sound of my heavy boot crunching a pine cone startled Mora, and she looked up at me. A dollop of green laver was stuck on her pale chin. Her expression changed from a look of nervousness to a look of annoyance when she realized it was just me.

"Oh, Unfortunate Ursula Underwood, what do you want?"

"It's ironic for a woman sitting on a tree stump nervously consuming free bread to call me unfortunate, innit?" I retorted.

"That's why you're here then? Retribution? You delight in seeing me this way don't you, Unfortunate?"

"I do," I admitted and peered over her. "I do delight in this very much."

"I may be eating mission food, but I'm still better off than you. I still have my looks. And you still have, well, *yours*," she scoffed.

"If that's what you want to believe, Mora, so be it."

We watched one another in awkward silence for a moment before she finished the last bite of toast and brushed the crumbs from her face.

"Well, Unfortunate? Are you going to just stand there and stare at me all day?"

I shook my head.

"You're strange. Always have been," Mora jeered and stood from the stump. "What's that on your face? Bruising? How *unfortunate*! Who laid into you?"

"Why aren't you home, Mora? Why aren't you back on Gaius Hill with your pa? You've been downtown all this time, only a few miles from a safe, comfortable life? Why?"

"Wouldn't you love to know? Wouldn't you love to relish in my sordid tale?"

"I may find a sliver of satisfaction at your lot in life, but I would not relish in your misfortune."

"You want to know why I'm here, Unfortunate Ursula Underwood? Ask your sister's beau. He can enlighten you."

"Thaddeus?" I asked.

"How many beaus does your tart of a sister have? Of

course I'm speaking of Thaddeus! You were never quite bright were you?"

"What does Thad have to—"

"You've wasted enough of my time." She shoved me to the side and walked toward the coliseum.

"I'll never understand why you loathe me so, Mora. Since we were little girls, you've had such strong contempt for me—teasing, bullying and relentless degradation. I can think of no single incident in which I've deserved it!"

Mora remained silent, stomped through the pine needles and eventually disappeared into the gaping hole at the back of the coliseum. I stood silently in the trees for a few moments before following.

When I returned to the soup kitchen, I was relieved to see Pype conversing with Mr. Gunnar in the gray light basking through the torn roof. I softly touched the warm bruises on my face and hoped they were still somewhat concealed by the loose powder.

"Ursula?" He grinned at me and nodded at the back of the building. "Where are you coming from?"

"I've just come from a walk through the woods. Where've you been?"

"I was making another batch of laverbread for tomorrow's breakfast. It's quite delicious. Do you fancy it?"

"I've never fancied seaweed," I said.

"It is my father's favorite," he paused. "Your face, Ursula? Are you bruised?"

"Oh." I reached up and touched my brow. "I slipped on a patch of clear ice in front of my apartment. I'm quite alright."

"You took a hard fall?"

"Yes," I answered. "It's no worry, though. It's healing."

"You should have let me know. I would have—"

"Pay it no mind, Pype. I said I'm quite alright."

"Alright." He nodded but still looked concerned.

"Well," I said. "I just thought I would stop by and see that you're well."

"Why wouldn't I be?" He smiled.

"I keep thinking of the incident with Thad the other night. I worry that he will be out to get you. Revenge is his only strong suit."

"I'm not very concerned with that, Ursula. However, I appreciate that you are."

"It would be my fault if something were to happen—"

"Go with me over the bridge this evening, Ursula," he interrupted. "We will browse the boardwalk and dine at Paius. Have you been there? They offer leftovers to southerners at a reasonable price. Even though days old, their cranberry cake is delicious."

"I can't, Pype." I shook my head.

"Oh you'd enjoy it," he pleaded and smiled.

"I mean I cannot go over the bridge," I answered. "I've no more visits this month."

"Well that's a relief. I assumed you just did not want to spend time with me."

"No." I blushed.

"Then we'll go to the diner on 7th? You will join me there?"

I drowned in his coffee-colored eyes and accepted his offer, although I knew I should not. I enjoyed my comfortable life and would have been plenty content to share salmon with my cat by the fire that evening. However, I rarely took my own advice.

Bronwyn was surprised to see me enter the diner at 77 7th Street at 7 PM on Saturday evening. I could see her thinking intensely and pondering if she'd gone crazy or if I had.

"Ursula, it is Saturday, innit? Have I gone mad? It is Saturday, yeah?" she called from behind the shiny aluminum counter as cigarette smoke circled her yellow hair.

"It is, Bronwyn." I smiled and nodded to Pype sitting alone at a booth not far from the one I frequented every Sunday.

Bronwyn responded with a wide grin and a wink.

"Hello," I greeted Pype. He stood from the red vinyl booth while I slid into the seat across from him.

Although I was already chilled from the air conditioning, I removed my wool coat to reveal a navy turtleneck sweater and cream slacks. I'd worn my hair in a soft bun at the nape of my neck, donned my mother's pearls and applied plenty of powder to conceal my wounds. I had worried what to wear to dinner with Pype and was unsure if sharing a meal with him was considered courting or if we were just dining as friends, as Finley and I often did before he was plagued with ulcers. However, I'd never worn pearls for Finley.

"You look lovely this evening," Pype interrupted my thoughts.

"Thank you." I blushed and noticed that he'd worn a starched beige shirt with tortoiseshell buttons and brown trousers. Finley certainly did not wear such church attire when we came to the diner together either. "You do as well."

"I was unsure how to dress," he replied. "Is this time spent together romantic in nature or merely two friends breaking bread?"

My mouth dropped at the possibility that this man could read my thoughts. "I'm unsure, Pype." I laughed.

Bronwyn walked over to us. Her plum lips were parted in a smile, and her chubby face looked quite delighted that I was in the company of a man.

"Would you like the usual, Ursula?"

"No." I pulled the tattered menu from between the glass spice shakers and glanced at it. "I think I'll go with the falafel and a side of hummus tonight, Bronwyn."

"Wonderful! But it is quite uncommon for you, innit, Ursula?" She chuckled and wrote on her small notepad. "And for you, Sir?"

"What's that you usually get here, Ursula?" Pype looked to me.

"Every Sunday. 7:07. Pulled pork and apple grilled cheese

with crisps and blackcurrant tea. Table 7. Ursula Underwood," Bronwyn answered as Pype cocked his head quizzically.

"That sounds just fine," he finally said. "Pulled pork and apple grilled cheese with crisps and blackcurrant tea sounds just fine. Saturday." Then he looked to the number protruding from the napkin holder. "Table 4. Ursula Underwood and Pype Tyburn."

Bronwyn cackled before she wiped her sweaty brow and said, "Tabb will be astonished to know that you are here but that request isn't from you, Ursula!" Then she left us alone.

I timidly tapped my thumbs together as Pype fidgeted with his tortoiseshell cufflink. The silence was unbearable. I mulled over dialogue in my mind, but my mouth failed to produce intelligent sound.

"Rather awkward, innit?" Pype mumbled.

I chuckled. "Funny how our conversations never lulled at the soup kitchen or on our walk about town, and now we are at a loss."

"Perhaps we should entertain the question that I raised earlier?"

"What's that?"

"Is this meeting romantic in nature or no?" He squirmed tensely in the red booth.

"Pype, I don't—" I stammered. "I feel quite embarrassed at the query."

"Ursula," he paused. "I apologize. I hope you know it isn't my intention to make you uncomfortable. But may I tell you how I view this meeting and you can opt not to respond?"

I nodded.

"As I told you the other evening on our walk, I have grown quite fond of you." He shifted his eyes to his large hands resting on the ivory table. "I find you refreshing."

"That's kind, Pype," I said as my heart fluttered beneath my sweater. It fluttered and leapt the same way it did the day I met Prentice Fawkes here many years ago. "I am unsure how to respond as I do not have much experience with romance."

"There was a girl on the north side. Manon Dee." He smiled. "I cared for her deeply."

"Was she beautiful?" I asked, somewhat jealous at the glow on his face as he reminisced of her.

"Very." He nodded. "She was coveted by many. Her eyes were blue as the Welshlynn Sea and her hair the color of the noonday sun. Striking, Manon was. I assume she still is."

"She sounds lovely," I replied resentfully.

"But Manon's beauty, like so many others, merely resided on the surface. She possessed superficial beauty. Her heart was dark. Her motives were clouded by anger. She loved me, I know, but she was vehemently opposed to my mission to come here. And she wasn't unsupportive merely because she would long for me when I was gone. She was blinded by hatred and prejudice. She was unwavering in her belief that everyone south of the Winnow deserved poverty and even death."

I remained silent and picked at my fingernails.

"Your beauty, Ursula," he said as I looked up to him. "Your beauty isn't merely outward. You're stunning through and through. You speak truth and radiate love and kindness. You're meek and gentle. You are oblivious to how beautiful you truly are, Ursula. That's what I find refreshing."

My face flushed again. "Now I truly am embarrassed, Pype Tyburn."

"That's a product of your modesty."

I sighed. "Your words are kind yet hard for me to digest. I've never viewed myself in the manner you've just described. There is so much that you do not know about me, Pype. Like your friend on the north side, I also struggle with hatred and dark thoughts and desires. Your opinion of me is kind, but it is not accurate."

"Don't we all possess both darkness and light? Which spectrum people thrive on is always evident. You, Ursula, you thrive on light. That is the epitome of beauty."

I smiled as Bronwyn sat two steaming cups of blackcurrant

tea before us. "Tabb had to peek out of the kitchen to see that I was truthful in my declaration that your friend here ordered the pork and crisps, Ursula." She giggled. "It'll be out in two shakes."

"Thank you, Bronwyn," I said without breaking my gaze at Pype's dark eyes and strong cheekbones.

"Tell me more about you, Ursula Underwood. Include the dark with the light. My opinion of you will not waver."

"I relish in the suffering of the man who murdered my father," I blurted. "I find great joy at his struggle. I, too, find the same satisfaction in the hardship of the girl who caused me much dismay years ago and calls me unfortunate. I consider my sister to be a burden. I covet life on the northern side. I am not content. That's my darkness, Pype."

"That's your darkness?"

"Shameful, innit?"

"Realistic, yes, but shameful? Certainly not, Ursula! You possess ill will toward those who've wronged you. Your sister's antics have tired you. You desire an abundant life. That isn't darkness, dear girl. That's humankind."

"I'm predictable. I was recently told by a wise man not to be predictable."

"You are too stern with yourself. You're meek and gentle with everyone but Ursula."

"There's another sin, but I can't bear to admit it to you, Pype. It's egregious and no one knows about it but my mother and Lolly."

"You won't tell me?"

"I won't, Pype. I cannot. I only mention it so that you will fully understand that I am not the beautiful person that you claim I am."

"I can't imagine you've done anything so horrible that it would tarnish your splendor," he answered as Bronwyn approached our table.

"Grilled cheese and crisps for the mister and falafel and hummus for the lady." She set our plates before us. "Can I get you

~ 128 ~

anything else? More tea perhaps?"

"This will be fine, Bronwyn," I answered as Pype nodded in agreement. "Thank you."

"The food looks delightful." He examined his plate, wide-eyed.

"I've fancied pulled pork and apple grilled cheese since I was a child. Tabb's recipe resembles my mother's. I recollect many fond memories with each bite."

"Why didn't you fancy it tonight?" He chewed the warm, melted cheese.

"I'll have it tomorrow. As Bronwyn said, it's what I have every Sunday at Table 7."

"How did that tradition come to be?"

"My ma and I used to dine here every Sunday evening after chapel. Now I come here and speak to her every Sunday night on the payphone in the corner."

"Where is she? Your ma?" Pype wiped his mouth with his napkin and searched my face.

"I just cannot be with her now. That's all I have to say about that," I quickly retorted.

"I see." He nodded and returned his eyes to his plate. "The man who took your father's life— we passed his shack that day we discovered the family in the woods?"

"Yes. Oden Barmouth."

"I don't believe I've ever seen him at the soup kitchen," he said. "We should go to him."

"Go and see him?" I sipped my tea. "I am not ready to forgive him, Pype. I told you that my mother would love nothing more, but I'm not yet ready."

"You don't have to forgive him to talk to him. It seems to me that you simply need closure. Come face to face with the man who causes you so much anger. Confront it. There's great healing to be found in confronting pain."

"I couldn't." I shook my head.

"You could. We'll go together."

"Tonight?!"

"Soon, but not tonight. Tonight I want to ask of you another favor."

"That is?" I pulled apart the steaming fried chickpeas.

"I want you to draw my caricature."

"Oh! Pype, I couldn't!" I laughed.

"And why not?"

"It's merely a silly portrait. It's folly! What do you need with an exaggerated portrait of yourself? It's for children!"

"I hear you have great talent. Dennison tells me the youngsters on the boardwalk delight in your work. I'd like to delight in it as well."

"Pype." I sighed and shook my head. "All of my supplies are at home."

"Then that's where we'll go. Finish your hummus."

We exited the diner and stopped in front of the window stained with condensation to put on our coats. I slipped my hands inside the black leather gloves and before I could shove them into my pockets, Pype grabbed my left with his right. He gave it a squeeze as I looked up at him and grinned.

He asked, "The ice on the trees is quite beautiful, innit?"

I nodded. "I'm not keen on cold weather, but those dead limbs do seem to come to life again when they are coated in that sparkling frozen water."

"I once sat in a Runyon tree as it froze." He chuckled.

"You what?" I smirked while we walked along the dark, empty street.

"I often climbed the Runyon near the wheat field behind our home when I was a boy. It was my favorite place." He smiled. "From the highest branch, I could see for miles. The church steeple, the Winnow and the great plateau; all visible from that Runyon tree top. And one winter evening, after quarrelling with my father over something exceptionally petty, I escaped to that tree. I sat there for hours in the sprinkling rain as the temperature dropped, and it froze. It froze right there with me in it."

"It didn't, Pype!" I giggled.

"It did!" He looked down at me and snickered. "I was frozen solid to that branch. I could not come down for three days."

"You tell tales." I squeezed his gloved hand as our laughs echoed in the winter night.

When we reached my apartment, we both removed our shoes and gloves and hung our coats on the hall tree next to the door. I quickly scanned my home and became embarrassed at the clutter and cat hair on my bureau, the quilt haphazardly hanging over the back of my sofa and the rye crumbs on the kitchen counter.

"I'm not as tidy as you," I confessed.

"I know of no one who is, Ursula." Pype winked at me.

"Shall I fix you some tea?"

"I'm fine," he answered. "May I sit?"

"Oh, please do." I motioned toward the couch. "I'll just get my art supplies."

I retrieved my canvas sack of pencils and drawing parchment from the small closet near the door, carried it to the couch and sat next to Pype as he rolled up the sleeves of his cream shirt.

"Your home is quite cozy," he said. "And who is that fine specimen sleeping in the windowsill?"

"Oh." I grinned. "That's Garfunkel. Wretched soul, he is."

"He looks far from wretched. I'll wager he's a wonderful companion."

"You see where he is, don't you? He rarely comes near me unless I hold food in my hand or he's cold and requires my warmth."

"You've been together a long time?"

"A decade or so," I answered and nodded. "I'm not quite fond of cats, but he's managed to stick around. There's no reason to turn him out in the cold at this point. He keeps the mice away at least."

"I reason you'll be quite sad when that cat's time comes," Pype said.

"I suspect you're right," I agreed. "As I said, I hope you aren't expecting a great portrait to have matted and displayed in your home."

"That's exactly what I expect!"

"I'm afraid you'll be sorely disappointed." I pulled the sketch pad and pencils from the bag and sat them on the table next to the couch.

"Must I be perfectly still?"

"No." I looked at him and began drawing. "There are no instructions for caricatures. This isn't serious art."

"You are humble in every aspect, aren't you?"

"If you insist, Pype." I scratched the pencil across the paper.

"Have you loved another before, Ursula?" His question took me by surprise and caused my face to flush.

"You're consumed by romantic queries this evening, aren't you?"

"I am when in the company of a delightful and single woman."

"Pype, please." I shook my head. "For someone who has no intention of embarrassing me, you're doing a dreadful job."

"Forgive me yet again, Ursula."

"To answer your question," I said and sketched his fresh haircut, "I have loved before."

"Someone I may know?"

"Possibly." I nodded. "Prentice Fawkes."

Pype laughed loudly and slapped his knee. "Ursula! You joke!"

"No. You know him then?" I rested my pencil.

"Oh, I've seen him around. Sandy-haired fellow who works in sanitation? Fancies a chipmunk, doesn't he?"

I laughed. "I've never thought of that, but I guess he does."

"Of course he does with those chubby cheeks and enlarged front teeth!" He teased.

"Pype, really!" I continued to grin and shook my head. "That isn't kind."

"I'm sorry!" He gasped between laughs. "Well what happened? Tell!"

I shrugged. "I fancied him more than he fancied me. The rejection broke my heart. There's nothing more to tell."

"Oh, Ursula." His smile slowly faded. "Well, I consider your heartache a blessing. If you and Munk had married, I would not be here this evening now would I?"

I snickered and finished sketching the incredibly large ear. I moved on to the long nose and accentuated the smile lines on either side of his wide, beaming mouth. It seemed such a disservice to make folly of such a handsome face.

"How'd you get into this business of drawing caricatures?"

"Before the mill closed, there was a comic shop over on 6th Street. I spent a lot of time there while Ma did her shopping around town. There was a fascinating caricature hanging on the wall, drawn by a local artist named Dabney Silverchair. I would stare at that picture until Ma came back to get me. It was so humorous and whimsical and gave me such a cheerful feeling," I remembered aloud. "Well, one day Silverchair came into the comic shop while I was there. He was an old, wrinkled man with thinning black hair and a bent nose. He noticed me admiring that caricature and came over to speak to me. Said the man in the sketch with the wide, crossed eyes and pointed ears was his younger brother. I asked Silverchair to teach me to draw that way, and he generously obliged. We sat at a little wobbly table in the back of the comic shop every Tuesday afternoon while Ma bought groceries and picked up our Sunday clothes from the laundry, and old Silverchair with his creased, shaking hands taught me to draw. The comic shop's owner, Mr. Hassock, didn't even mind. He displayed a few of my caricatures on the wall next to Silverchair's picture until the shop closed."

"That's a lovely story."

"Well." I scribbled my initial at the bottom of the satirical picture and eyed it one more time. "I guess that's it."

"That was hasty! Let me see." He reached for the paper. I handed it over and anxiously bit my bottom lip.

"Ursula!" He glowed. "It's brilliant."

"I wouldn't—"

"Stifle your humbleness for a moment and accept my compliment! It truly is brilliant." He chuckled. "It's me, yet it isn't!"

"That's what most say when they see their caricature."

"Have you ever drawn anything else? Abstract?"

I quickly shook my head. "No."

"This requires great talent." He shook the drawing. "I'm certain you could sketch stunning things— landscapes, sunsets, that handsome cat in the windowsill."

I shrugged. "Perhaps."

"Positively!" he exclaimed. "You have no idea what a gift you are, Ursula. You truly have no idea. That's why I keep saying it."

"*A gift*?" I scoffed. "What exactly is the purpose in this praise, Pype? I have no desire to go through heartbreak yet again. You're the only man to declare such things about me. It makes me suspicious of your intentions. And it makes me suspicious of your intelligence," I crossly declared and put the colored pencils back into the canvas bag.

"My declarations should make you suspicious of others' intelligence. Perhaps I'm the only one smart enough to see what a treasure you are," he answered and stood from the couch with the portrait in his hand. "If I'm making you embarrassed and suspicious then perhaps I should go."

"Pype." I sighed, stood and then followed him to the hall tree where he was retrieving his coat. "It wasn't my intention to hurt your feelings. You have to understand. I've never heard a man use such glorifying adjectives to describe me. Prentice Fawkes?

That's all I've ever known of love, and it was one-sided. I've never been on the receiving end of romance. You must know that it is foreign to me."

"I realize that, Ursula." He nodded. "It's foreign for me to feel this way as well. I told you earlier that I cared for Manon, but it was a shallow affection. The liking I have for you is much more profound. I admire your outward beauty, but there are outwardly beautiful women everywhere. To find a woman with true inner beauty is what I find foreign. Forgive me if I have come on too strong." He stepped into his brown loafers next to the door.

"No apology necessary."

"Thank you for a lovely evening and a brilliant drawing." He looked at it in his hands before returning his eyes to me. "I'm certain that I sound repetitive, but you will ponder my question? You'll ponder whether our relationship is romantic in nature or merely friendship? Whatever your conclusion is satisfactory, as I covet both."

"Yes." I nodded.

"I knew I would find you when I came south." He slipped his coat over the starched shirt with the tortoiseshell buttons.

"What's that?"

"When I saw those little girls turned away from the grocer, a seed was planted within me to come here, but I struggled with the decision to cultivate that seed for some time. I told you I could not sleep. But one day the phone rang at the jewelry store. I answered and the kindest voice I'd ever heard, the voice of an angel, told me to come south. I was so confused and stammered into the phone, and the voice repeated, *Go south. You'll find a good thing there in a striking girl with fair skin and eyes like cocoa, but more importantly, her inner beauty will surpass all. Go south and she'll come to you. You possess a common cause. Go south. You'll sleep again.*"

My mother. My mother had made the call.

"I waited a long time for you to come to me, and I almost lost hope," he said. "I have yet to hear that voice again, but I want to thank it when I do. A guardian angel, you suppose, Ursula? You believe the Most High commands angels to guide us?"

I hesitated, my mouth open. "I'm certain," I finally said in almost a whisper.

Pype leaned in closely, wrapped his hand holding the caricature around my waist and gently kissed me. When he slowly pulled away, my lips were still parted and my eyes still closed.

"Good night, Ursula." He opened the door and disappeared down the hall.

THIRTEEN

On Sunday evening before returning to the diner with an appetite for pork and a list of questions for my mother, I decided to check on Finley. I rapped on his door in my usual way before entering the kitchen filled with the familiar and stout aroma of spiced tea.

"Finley?" I called.

"I'm in the back," he answered. "Come on in, Ursula."

I placed my coat on the kitchen table and walked down the narrow, dark hallway to Finley's bedroom at the rear of the home. His iron wheelchair was parked next to his bulky four-poster bed, and his gun was on the side table.

"Why've you retired so early?" I looked at him resting beneath the crisp, cream sheets with the tattered copy of Terrapin Greenlaw's novel next to him.

"I've felt quite ill today," he responded and pushed his glasses up his nose.

"Your ulcer?"

He nodded. "It's raging today. I haven't felt such intense burning before."

"You've any more of the licorice root and cabbage that I brought last week?" I sat on the edge of the bed, careful not to press his shriveled legs.

"I've no more licorice."

"I'll bring some more tomorrow, yeah? It helps?"

Finley inhaled sharply and clutched his stomach. "Yeah, it helps ease the pain. Not sure if it's enough, though."

"Finley, this cannot go on. Physician Tryce must bring you medicine from the north side! I am certain there are remedies that can cure you!"

"Physician Tryce is quite occupied. He's concerned with so many patients, including Pa."

"Has he yet gone north to obtain treatment for Mr. Farkas?"

Finley shook his head.

"Preposterous, Finley! What a shame that our only

physician has become so lax in his duties. Northern doctors refuse to treat us! If our health rests in Tryce's hands, we'll all be dead!"

"You mustn't say such things about Tryce, Ursula."

"Well, he was not much help to my own ma now was he?" I angrily crossed my arms.

"Ursula," Finley stammered, "you must-"

"I apologize. I know that you have great respect for Tallmadge Tryce, but I do hold a grudge."

"Understandable." Finley nodded.

"Perhaps I'll go north and retrieve your tablets myself− and Mr. Farkas'. I'll march right into the apothecary and demand them."

"The chemist oughtn't to dare serve you, Ursula! You think he'd just hand over tablets to a lowly southerner without a script? Even Tryce has a difficult time obtaining medication, and he has a physician's license. It would be a futile attempt on your part."

"Of course you're right, Finley." I shook my head. "It just angers me how we are made to suffer. I'm sorry the licorice has not healed you. I was sure-"

"Do not dare to apologize. You've done more for me than any other."

"So what shall we do then? Let you burn from the inside out? Shall I call Physician Tryce myself? Perhaps I could persuade him to give me the script−"

"Leave it be, Ursula." Finley twisted at the pain in his abdomen. "Leave it be."

"It saddens me to see you this way. You're my dearest friend, Finley."

"And you mine."

"Do you−" I laughed. "Do you remember the time we fooled the pedestrians crossing Hoorn Avenue? I purposely let go of your chair, and you sailed down Gaius Hill screaming for your life?"

Finley roared.

"Oh, Finley! You had ten or more chasing after you! I can

still envision Batilda Salley's short legs moving so quickly! She resembled a Corgi dog chasing after a ball! And plump Mr. Orrin dared not drop his pastry as he rolled after you, too!"

"Oh, Ursula!" Tears formed in Finley's eyes. "How angry they were when I finally halted at the bottom of the hill and began laughing uncontrollably! Mr. Orrin called me a bloody pillock and kicked the wheel of my chair! He would not look at me for years after that stunt."

"Fond memories, Finley." I wiped my eyes damp from happy tears. "Fond memories, indeed."

"We'll make more, Ursula," he assured me and locked his fingers with mine. "Physician Tryce will get the tablets I require, and we'll make more. Perhaps another run down Gaius Hill is what we both need to lift our spirits?"

"I'd fancy that, Finley." I patted his clammy hand. "Although I doubt Mr. Orrin would ever chase after you again."

"That's true," he replied. "Well, any other news?"

"Nothing much." I grinned and paused. "Except that, well, I may have found true love, Finley."

"Love? You've found love in whom, Ursula? Do tell!" Finley sat up straight in the bed.

"It's the man from the soup kitchen. I've mentioned him. Pype Tyburn."

"The fellow who came south to help the hungry?"

"That's him." I nodded.

"He treats you well?"

I glowed at the thought of Pype. "He's so incredibly kind, Finley. He's complimented me in ways that I've never imagined. He believes me to be beautiful. He makes me feel like a schoolgirl. Can you imagine an old spinster feeling like a schoolgirl?"

Finley smiled. "And you return his affection?"

"I don't want to." I leaned against the bedpost. "I have fought it with all of my being, but I am beginning to care for him. Not only do I find his words to be satisfying, but he's incredibly handsome as well! That's quite shallow, innit?"

"Oh, dear friend, I am truly happy for you."

"I'm just terrified he's going to break my heart. What if he follows in the footsteps of Prentice? I could not bear it."

"He left a northern life to come here, didn't he? That is proof of what a good man he is. Such good men do not break hearts."

"I hope," I said.

"Don't let fear guide you. Do not let it deprive you of a beautiful relationship with this fellow. Don't let fear deprive you of the happiness you deserve."

"After 33 years, there is finally a man− a kind, decent, good man− who values me despite my plain appearance and dark secrets."

"Ursula Underwood, you are quite *fortunate*."

When I pulled open the heavy door of the diner, the air conditioner blew the flurries that had settled on the shoulders of my coat to the floor. As I shook the remainder from my sleeves, I noticed Galvan and Chester mumbling quietly over their plates. I paced over to them.

"Good evening, gentlemen."

"Evening, Ursula," their hoarse, gruff voices spoke in unison.

"Are we to acknowledge the secret between us?"

"No," Chester responded quickly. "We certainly are not."

"Agreed." Galvan shoveled mashed sweet potatoes into his mouth while a small orange portion settled in his beard.

"Well, I may not agree with the demise of those three men, but I do want to express my gratefulness."

"Don't speak of it," Chester replied.

Galvan motioned for me to lean in close to him and said quietly, "If anyone inquires about that night, you know nothing, Ursula. Tell me. You know nothing."

"I know nothing, Galvan." I leaned away from the table.

"Is there anything else you wish to discuss about the

situation?" Chester asked. "If no, then we do not admit it ever again. Understood?"

"I've no other opinions on the matter," I answered. "And I know nothing."

"Evening, Ursula." Chester resumed cutting the loin on his plate.

I nodded and walked toward Table 7.

"Tea'll be right out," Bronwyn called from the aluminum counter as she wrote on her notepad.

"Thank you," I said before sliding into the booth and focusing again on Galvan and Chester in the otherwise empty restaurant.

It was common knowledge that Galvan Montagne possessed a vile temper. Although he'd always been kind to me and had even repaired Ma's air conditioning at no charge several heat spells ago, rumors of his ability to be easily annoyed preceded him. I did not believe that Galvan was an evil man but rather a man who filled a void with anger. The void, of course, was the loss of his job at the mill. He'd served as supervisor, controlled the furnace and knew all there was to know about steel. When his trade was taken from him, it was replaced with resentment.

Galvan's wife, Clem, surely did not improve matters. She was known to nag and badger anyone within earshot and unfortunately, Galvan received the brunt of it. Her relentless harassing had only intensified his crossness. I pitied him and overlooked the grumpiness in his voice when he spoke to me.

"Did you enjoy your company last night?" Bronwyn interrupted my thoughts and sat the teacup on the table before me. "He seemed like a right nice fellow. Handsome chap, as well."

I grinned. "He is right nice, Bronwyn. I enjoyed his company very much."

"He reminded me of my Waynick with those dreamy brown eyes, dark hair and tall build. I mourn that man daily." Her face softened. "The boy is not local is he? I don't recall watching him come up from a child."

"He's not." I stirred my tea. "He came from the north."

"He did?" she exclaimed. "Why would he do that?"

"He came to help others, Bronwyn. He runs the soup kitchen. He's a decent man."

"Certainly he must be." She nodded. "Well, I reckon you'll have the usual tonight?"

"Yes, ma'am, I will. Extra crisps."

"It'll be out in roughly seven minutes." The phone rang. "But you already know that."

"Hello, dear."

"Ma."

"Good things this week?"

"I would prefer we start with other business."

"And that is, dear?"

"Pype Tyburn, Ma."

"How are you getting along with him?"

"We are getting along just fine. He fancies me beautiful inside and out. He fancies me just fine."

"Oh, Ursula—"

"Ma, you coerced him to come south, didn't you? You placed a phone call and told him he would find me here. You told him that I'd help him— that we possessed a common cause. That is how it went, innit?"

Ma remained silent.

"Why would you meddle that way, Ma? I have made it abundantly clear to you over the years that I have no desire to long for a man and risk being heartbroken. I understand that you guide me to help those who bear incredible burdens, but why would you do this? Why would you place him in my path? Place me in his?"

"Because you bear an incredible burden. As does he, Ursula."

"And that is?"

"He's never known true love. You've never known true love, either. Why wouldn't I bring you together? He's a wonderful

~ 142 ~

man, Ursula. Surely you know that by now. Have I done wrong? Have I sent you someone unworthy of your love?"

"No, Ma," I stuttered, "but you know how cautious I am when it comes to romantic affairs. You know that Prentice Fawkes–"

"Enough, Ursula!" Ma shouted in an unfamiliar and stern tone. "Enough drivel concerning Prentice Fawkes! Do you believe you're the first to suffer through adolescent heartbreak? Of course you are not! You've so much to release, Ursula– anger, condemnation, which we've discussed, but also the ill will you possess toward love just because a young man didn't return your affection 15 years ago!"

"Ma–"

"You know the love I possess for you, Ursula. Would I ever encourage you to enter someone's life if I knew they were going to harm you? I know Pype Tyburn's heart. There is nothing to fear concerning him. Now quit your grumbling! You know as well as I do that you are ecstatic to receive this affection from Pype! Yet you act angry that I brought you together!"

Right as always, Ma was.

I blurted unexpectedly, "You're so incredibly perfect and whole. You love unconditionally. You forgive effortlessly and know what I need even before I do. It annoys me at times."

"Where am I, Ursula? Are you aware?"

"Of course I am aware."

"Being here is the sole reason that I am made whole, am able to love unconditionally, forgive effortlessly and give sound advice. Surely you remember that I have not always been this way? Do you remember your childhood, Ursula? Do you remember the malice I harbored for the man who took your father from me? Do you remember the hatred I felt for my own mother after our meeting in Wheatsand, when I drug you and Lolly there in homemade dresses? Do you remember the harsh words I spoke of Thad because he was harming my little girl? Do you remember how I soaked my feet each night and asked you to rub ointment on my back after scrubbing Kinneman's floors for hours on end? Do you remember finding me on the kitchen floor crying due to my many burdens? Do you remember me when I was not whole, Ursula?"

"I do, Ma." I wiped a lone tear from my nose. "But I remember your strength to keep going."

"I possessed strength because strength is needed to survive there. You possess that same strength, Ursula. You are still there on the south side of the Winnow in bondage and surrounded by poverty. You long for your father each day while his killer lives only a piece across the woods from you. You cannot dissolve your memories of Mora Sloane's hurtful antics. You cannot cease worrying for your sister who lives at the hand of a wretched man. You live with the world's burdens, Ursula, and I am well-aware of it. Of course I coerce you to good things for your neighbors. I urge you to forgive and replace intolerance with acceptance. I suggest you do these things because I see now— now that I am here— that life goes by too quickly to live any other way. I want you to live the best life you can and love the best way you know how and do as much good as you can because I see the grand scheme now, Ursula. Of course I'm aware that it is difficult for you, but it certainly is not unattainable! You have the strength to not only survive there, Ursula, but to thrive. You must not be annoyed because I am here."

"I have used the incorrect word. I am not annoyed. I am envious."

"You must not be envious, either. You have too much purpose there. You'll be like me when we are joined together again, but that time is not now." Ma sighed. "Take my advice, Ursula, or don't. I love you and want you to make good decisions, but I'll not force you to do so. If you do not want a relationship with Pype Tyburn then end it, Ursula. If you do not want to make peace concerning Oden Barmouth then continue to spy on him and hate him from a cinderblock porch. If you want to spend valuable time despising Mora Sloane for the rest of your days, do it. If you want to wallow in pity over your southern address or your adolescent heartbreak then continue. You have free will."

"You're right. I know you are. I act such a fool sometimes. Just as Barton Huxley believed that his destitution was punishment for his sin, I believe that unhappiness and loneliness are just punishments for mine. I don't think I deserve Pype's affection. I shouldn't even be allowed these sacred conversations with you. I wallow in pity over Oden Barmouth and Mora and living south. I wallow in pity as recompense for my wrongs. I know it's absurd." I exhaled. "On and on and on I go. My constant deliberating is exhausting to not only me but to those around me. What should I do? What shouldn't I do? What is right? Who should I help? What sins should I forget? When will I let go of my guilt? My mind is constantly bombarded with these questions, and I am beat for it, Ma. I've lived these last three years punishing myself with worry. Your advice is so simple and freeing. I analyze entirely too much. My way of thinking is tiring, and it is time to end."

"You see, Ursula? You're growing. Love is healing you. My love, Pype's love and even your own love. Love yourself, dear daughter. You're so worthy of it. You do not deserve the punishments that you inflict upon yourself."

"There's something I must tell you," I said reluctantly and quietly. "Three men were killed at the hands of Barton Huxley, Chester and Galvan."

"Whatever for, Ursula?" Ma gasped as I noticed Chester and Galvan's booth was now empty.

"They were not good men. They harassed Chester and Galvan and then kicked me around, Ma. I'm quite alright, but Barton, Chester and Galvan defended me and, well, those northern men are buried in the woods now."

"Tuesday evening?"

"Yes, Ma," I said.

"I knew you were in danger, Ursula. I felt it. I felt uneasy for the first time since I've been away. I did not feel completely whole at the time."

"But you did not know specifics?"

"No," she answered. "I did not know why I felt that way. I just knew something was wrong. I began to pray for you. It was placed so heavily on my heart to pray."

"Barton Huxley says their deaths are justifiable. He says they were evil men and not repentant at all. I argued with him that there is light each one of us. I argued that they should not have taken those northern men's lives. What do you think?"

"Dear." Ma respired. "It is not for me to judge who is or is not repentant. It is certainly not for me to declare that murder is justified."

"But people can be evil through and through?"

"Yes, Ursula," she answered. "You know they can."

"And we should help them anyway?"

"We should exude love and kindness to all, even the unworthy. Our mercy may be the very thing to help them change."

"Were Barton, Galvan and Chester wrong then?"

"I cannot judge them either, Ursula."

"Oh, Ma!" I exclaimed. "I wish you would be clearer. Just tell me the right way to feel about this!"

"Let me be clear now then, Ursula," she said. "You are exhausting yourself with queries again. You do what you can do, and do not be concerned with others. Love, serve and live. It's really that simple. You fret and analyze entirely too much. You just said so yourself."

"Yes, Ma. Again, you're right. I suppose old habits die hard yeah?"

"Each morning when you wake, make a conscious effort to find joy in the day. Find joy in the arms of Pype Tyburn. Find joy in helping others whether or not you deem them worthy. Find joy despite the circumstances around you. And quit begging for answers that you aren't meant to know. Remember that the Most High is also The One. He's the only one who requires answers, and He already has them."

"Yes. And Papa?"

"You know I can't."

"Yes, Ma."

"Go do good things, dear. I love you. Always."

"Always."

The sound of glass dishes hitting the floor radiated throughout the diner. Then I heard Bronwyn exclaim from the kitchen, "I'm quite alright, Tabb!"

"Bron, have a seat here. I'll get you some cold tea."

"I told you I'm quite alright. I'm just so warm," Bronwyn responded as I poked my head through the swinging kitchen doors.

"Ursula, stand here with Bron while I fix her something cool!" Tabb waved for me to walk over to a peaked Bronwyn leaned against the massive sink.

"What's the matter?" I rushed next to her.

"Stop all this fuss!" Bronwyn screeched. "I just got quite warm and dizzy. I'm alright. It's after 7:07. We must get your food on the table, Ursula. We must-"

"Enough, Bronwyn," I said and pulled a stool from the corner. "Sit here now."

"If your crisps sit too long, they will no longer be crisp." She eased herself onto the seat and patted her perspiring forehead with her apron.

"Drink!" Tabb rushed over and shoved a tin cup of clean water into her pudgy hands.

"Oh, Tabb, the way you fuss!"

"He's right, Bronwyn. You should rest here and hydrate."

"I was just," she faltered and placed the cup to her lips. "I was just warm for a spell. It's nothing to fuss over."

"You are always warm!" Tabb laughed in an attempt to ease the tension. "While I am frying crisps and steaming vegetables, I am shivering because the air control is set so low. You are quite hot natured, eh, Bron?"

"Well." She gulped the rest of the liquid in the tin cup. "I am not sure what—"

"Bronwyn!" I watched her gasp for air. "Bronwyn, what's ever the matter? Are you warm again?"

She said nothing as her hairline soaked with sweat and the pink hue drained from her cheeks. She wheezed, and her eyes widened in fear and desperation.

"Bron! You need more drink? Bron?" Tabb yelped.

Suddenly Bronwyn, who seemed so full of life when she brought tea to my table only twenty minutes before, was sliding from the round stool. Her large body came down slowly. Tabb and I were unsuccessful in stopping her from dropping to the cold cement floor of the diner kitchen.

"Bron!" Tabb hovered over her. "Bron, stay with me now!"

I urgently pushed Tabb to the side and leaned over Bronwyn as the life slipped from her body. I pounded on her large chest and blew air into her smudged, ruby lips.

"Bronwyn!" I barked. "Breathe, Bronwyn."

Again and again I pumped her chest and blew into her mouth.

"We so graciously ask the Most High to allow this spirit to stay with us longer," Tabb prayed quietly. "Stay with us longer."

Still I passed air from my lungs to hers.

"Allow this spirit to stay with us longer," he repeated over and over in a low, cracked voice.

When I realized that my efforts were futile, I stopped to stare at my friend lying motionless on the hard floor with her eyes closed and the pencil from her brow smeared. Beads of sweat still rested on her forehead.

"No, Ursula," Tabb whined. "Tell me no."

Tears clouded my eyes and streamed down my nose. "I'm sorry, Tabb," I said. "I know nothing else to do."

"I will ring Tryce! He is at hospital on the corner-"

"No." I shook my head. "It's done."

"Allow this spirit to stay with us longer," Tabb pleaded again. "Allow this spirit to stay."

I looked at this large man, who had always seemed so

towering and invincible, sitting on the kitchen floor with tears soaking his cheeks. He wrapped his dark fingers around Bronwyn's pale hand and squeezed it gently.

"She was my family, Ursula." He sniffled. "The only family I have ever known, you know? She took me in when no one wanted me. She and Waynick loved me like I was their own."

Heartbroken, I wiped my eyes and stood to my feet. I silently thought for a moment before hurrying through the swinging kitchen doors and marching over to the payphone in the corner. As the air conditioner roared, I picked up the receiver and listened to the dial tone. I pressed 0 and waited for Magney Scullery to answer.

"Operator."

"Ms. Scullery, this is Ursula Underwood at the 7th Street Diner. Is there a way to call the number that just rang here not 20 minutes ago?"

"Evening, Ursula." She chewed taffy from her office in the warehouse on 4th Street. "I will attempt to trace it. You aren't aware of the call's origin?"

"No," I said. "I'm not certain the exact locale. Far away, I do know."

"You are aware that outgoing calls must be logged in the operator registry for the north side to review at any time? Did it possibly originate in Wheatsand?"

"It wasn't placed in Wheatsand. It was further."

"Withe? Swansea?"

"I'm certain it was much further, Ms. Scullery. Is there any possibility of tracing it?"

"Hold a moment, Ursula," she said before the line went silent. I could hear Tabb sniffling in the kitchen, along with his quiet pleas for Bronwyn's spirit to stay.

"Ursula, are you still with me?"

"Yes, Ms. Scullery."

"The number that came through is quite odd. I'm not familiar with it, but I believe I can place a call to it. Hold another moment, will you?"

"Yes. Thank you."

The quiet was interrupted by crackling ringing and static.

"Hello?"

"Ma?"

"Ursula, how did you find-"

"No matter, Ma! I need help. Bronwyn is gone, and Tabb is pleading to the Most High. Will you ask Him, as well, Ma? Please?"

"Ursula, I cannot make such a request. I cannot-"

"She is all that Tabb has. He will certainly succumb to depression and be along shortly after her! She's the only friend or family he has, Ma! Please! His pain is great!"

"I must not-"

"Do this for me, as well, Ma. The diner will cease without Tabb and Bronwyn. It will be just another destitute building. No one will step up to keep it going. No one will take on the burden of purchasing ingredients for the menu from the northern side! Bronwyn and Tabb have devoted most of their lives to keeping this place open, and what a special place it is for me! Please do this. Just send a prayer for her. Your prayers bear much weight."

"As do yours and Mr. Zaxby's, Ursula."

"Yes, but will you plead as well?"

Ma sighed. "Yes, Ursula. I will right away. I love you. Always."

"Always."

I banged the phone back into its cradle and scurried to the kitchen where Tabb was rocking back and forth on the floor. He held Bronwyn's yellow head in his lap while tears streamed down his dark face.

"Allow this spirit to stay with us longer," he cried. "Allow this spirit..."

I crouched down next to him and put my arms around his wide shoulders. "Allow this spirit to stay with us longer," we closed our eyes and said in unison until the roar of a loud gasp filled the room.

"Bron!" Tabb shouted and gently lifted her head. "Bron! Are you with me? Praise the Most High! He heard our plea!"

She opened her dazed eyes and stared at us both for a moment. "What's ever the matter with you peering at me like that? I was just a bit warm! I told you I'm quite alright."

"Bronwyn!" I cackled. "Bronwyn! Are you really alright?"

"Quite." She leaned up. "What am I doing here on the floor? Did I slip?"

"Oh, Bron!" Tabb laughed heartily. "What a scare you gave us!"

"I had the strangest dream," she said as we helped her steady on her feet. "Your ma was there, Ursula. I saw my dear friend Geraldine."

"You saw Ma, Bronwyn?"

"Her hair was aglow. Nearly as glowing as mine!" She chuckled and patted the damp and golden strands framing her plump face. "She did not say a word. Only looked at me gently the way she always did when she brought you wee girls in for Sunday night supper after church."

I smiled.

"You can stand?" Tabb asked, concerned.

"Of course I can, Tabb! I was just quite warm. I told you that! Now let us get these broken dishes and mess cleaned up. Make a new batch of crisps for Ursula, Tabb. It must be a sight past 7:07 now."

"Thank you, Ma," I whispered.

FOURTEEN

On Monday morning the abrupt sound of banging echoed throughout my apartment. When my eyes finally focused, I noticed through my bedroom window that it was merely dawn. I could not conceive who would be beating on my door so early.

The pounding was relentless as I groggily rose from the bed, put on my slippers and robe and shuffled into the living room. If Leo Magnus had come over with data entry in tow, demanding that I begin work at dawn, I would give him what for!

"Coming! Coming!" I yelled over the loud noise and threw open the door. "What's ever the matter?"

Leo Magnus did not stand at my threshold. Irwell Bleddyn stood there instead in his dark blue squad uniform and peaked hat.

"Ursula, may I come in?" He motioned his baton inside.

"Well, good morning, Irwell. What brings you here at only half past sunrise?" I shut the door behind him.

Irwell silently examined my living room. When I saw him patrolling the streets, I was always reminded of the time he slipped on ice when we were children and knocked out his two front teeth. Twenty years later, he'd better grown into the prosthetics, although they still visibly protruded through his lips even when his mouth was closed.

"Have you heard the news, there, Ursula?" He casually swayed the baton back and forth.

"I've been asleep for hours, Irwell. I've heard nothing this morning but my door's abuse."

"You've not spoken to Lolly?"

"Irwell, what has happened?" I became concerned and walked toward him.

"Thaddeus was found in Dugald Alley this morning. Dead."

"Dead?" I gasped. "You must be mistaken! Passed out drunk I assume, but certainly not dead!"

"Dead as yesterday, Ursula. The rats had already taken hold of him. Fancied something other than Kestral's kale, I suppose."

I grimaced. "Lolly? Is she alright?"

"Your sister is fine, Ursula. She's at the station now being questioned by Whitchurch. What she knows, he'll soon know. He's a bloody genius at extracting the truth."

"What are you implying, Irwell? You believe Lolly had a part in this?"

"I'm not certain, Ursula." He pointed to my couch. "Sit with me a spell?"

"Ye-yes," I stammered and sat down next to him as a sleepy Garfunkel entered the living room and stretched from his slumber.

"It is common knowledge that you and Thaddeus were not the best of friends." Irwell took a notepad from the pocket of his navy coat. "Where were you between 9 last evening and 3 this morning?"

"You're serious, Irwell? Now you are suggesting that I had something to do with Thad's demise?"

"I've worked with Thad a long time, Ursula. I cannot tell you how often he groaned about you. Yes, I have to admit that he was a sight hard to get along with, and I've never agreed with his stance concerning you, but you have to understand that I must question everyone who deems to be a suspect."

"If you are looking to question people who had a cross word with Thad at some point, then you will be right busy interrogating the entire south side, Irwell."

"Your whereabouts, Ursula?"

"Well," I remembered aloud as my heart skipped, "I left the diner around 8 last night, came straight home, read this book." I picked up the copy of Porthcawl's *Cloud of Witnesses* on the side table. "And then I retired. I just woke when you banged on my door."

"I see," he said and scribbled my alibi on the notepad. "When was the last time you spoke to Thaddeus?"

"I am not sure." I sighed and darted my eyes around the room. "Last week I suppose. I saw him…"

My voice trailed off when I recalled his altercation with Pype outside the ale house. Pype! Had he done this? Had Pype killed Thaddeus Jessop? In self-defense?

"Yes, Ursula?" Irwell interrupted my thoughts.

"He was, was," I stuttered. "He was stumbling out of the ale house. We had words."

"And?"

"We had words, and I left. I have not seen him since," I said.

"That is all that happened? You're completely certain?"

I nodded.

"Are you forgetting that your suitor pelted him in the jaw that evening, Ursula? Has that detail slipped your mind?"

"What, Irwell?" I pretended to be confused.

"I worked with the man!" Irwell exclaimed and stood to his polished shoes. "He came into work the following day with a cracked jaw, Ursula! Said your beau assaulted him right there in the street for reasons unknown. I know things, Ursula, and it is futile to withhold information from me. We are speaking of the demise of an official South Side Squadron member! This is quite serious! The penalty is death!"

"I know!" I stood as well. "But I did not kill Thad Jessop! I had nothing to do with it. He loathed me, as I did him, but I am no murderer! I will repeat it to you and Whitchurch and anyone else who interrogates me!"

"Very well. Your friend at the soup kitchen? Where was he last night?"

"You will have to ask him, Irwell. I do not know."

Irwell calmed. "I apologize for raising my voice, Ursula. You will inform me if you learn anything?"

"Of course I will. What of my sister? May I go and see her at the station?"

"She is not allowed visitors at this time. I am sure she will contact you when she is released."

"Yes, Irwell. Thank you."

Irwell moved toward the door. Before exiting, he looked back to me and said, "Perhaps Lolly will lead quite a joyful life now."

I nodded.

After I paced the apartment and my nerves settled a bit, I had a cup of blackcurrant tea with toast and boysenberry jam. I left for Leo's later than usual, and when I reached his office on Pascass, I was smothered by the heat radiating from the brick stove in the center of the building and the strong odor of mint tea. Mrs. Inchcape sat behind a mound of papers on her oversized desk in the corner of the large room and clacked her long fingernails against the typewriter keys.

Mrs. Inchcape was in her late forties— petite with thick black bangs that rested right above her eyebrows. She owned rectangle glasses in a plethora of colors, and today she wore jade eyewear to match her green cardigan sweater. I had always found it quite humorous that her husband, Caldwell, resembled her so with his own short stature, heavy bangs and rectangle spectacles.

"Morning, Ursula. You draggin' today?" Her accent was as thick as if she'd grown up on the eastern shore of the Welshlynn Sea.

"A bit," I responded.

"No doubt due to the news, eh?" Her eyes shifted to me from beneath the glasses.

"You've heard?"

"Oh yes, dear. Everyone has. Awful shame, innit?" She searched my face.

"It's an awful shame my sister is being interrogated this very moment."

"Everyone knows Lolly ain't harmed that boy," she replied adamantly. "She don't have the heart. Everyone knows 'at!"

~ 156 ~

"Everyone but Whitchurch."

"Whitchurch is a right nit, ain't he? Lead investigator my foot! I can think of ten other men to serve that position better, including my Caldwell. My Caldwell would not even waste his time interviewing your sister to such an extent. He'd know within five seconds of talking to her that she is innocent. Whitchurch just badgers suspects until half of them confess out of exhaustion. That's what my Caldwell says."

"Yes, Mrs. Inchcape," I said. "Well, I best get my data entry. Where is Mr. Magnus?"

"Ain't sure, Ursula," she said. "He celebrated his birthday yesterday evening. Probably had too much ale and is still sleeping in his bed with all those herding dogs of his."

"I'll have these done by weekend," I said and picked the stack from her cherry desk.

"Good luck to your sister, Ursula. I hope she won't confess out of fatigue. We all know what a louse Thad Jessop was. Many would like to see his head on a stick. I reckon your sister loved him and wouldn't aim to harm him no matter what he done to her."

"I reckon you're correct."

I shuffled down the street and noticed over the towering stack of papers in my arms the way people were observing me. All of the south side must have known about Thad's death, and they also knew my sister was a suspect. Possibly they believed me to be a suspect as well. The suspicion in their eyes was evident.

"Ursula!"

I whipped around to see my sister running toward me with swollen, damp eyes. "Lolly! I was just on my way to see you!"

I dropped the stack of bound papers to the cobblestone and took her into my arms.

"You're alright, yeah?"

"Yeah." She nodded and sniffled. "Thad is dead, Ursula. He's gone."

"I know, Lolly. Irwell told me this morning. Everyone

knows." We pulled away.

"I didn't do it, Ursula."

"Of course you didn't!"

"That Whitchurch badgered me for hours!" She rubbed her tired eyes and shook her head. "Woke me in the middle of the night and hauled me down to the station. He said they have sound evidence that I did it, but I did not! I loved him, Ursula. I loved Thad so. I could never hurt him."

"I know." I patted her shoulder as tears poured from her hazel eyes.

"Who would do this? Who harbored so much hate to kill him? Why not just leave him battered in the alley? Why stab him multiple times? Why so heinous?"

"They will find who did this, Lolly. He was a member of the squadron. They won't rest until his killer is found."

"You'll be truthful with me, yeah?" She batted wet eyelashes at me and pulled her dingy corduroy coat tightly around her body.

"Of course."

"You had nothing to do with this, did you? What about your friend at the soup kitchen? The one who hit Thad?"

"No, Lolly! It's no secret that I loathed Thad, but I'm not capable of this! You know that, don't you?"

"I do." She nodded. "But your friend? The one who fancies you? He couldn't-"

"Pype isn't capable of this, either. He only hit Thad that evening by the ale house to defend me. Thad was saying degrading things about me. Pype merely came to my aid."

"What if Thad was saying horrible things about you last night? What if your friend came to your aid yet again, but this time with a knife? That is possible, innit?"

"No, Lolly." I grabbed her by the shoulders. "Pype and I had nothing to do with this, alright? You won't plant that scenario in Whitchurch's mind, either, yeah? There's no truth to it."

"Yeah," she said. "I think I will go home and freshen up a

bit. Have something to eat, too. I will call on you later."

"You shouldn't be alone now, Lolly. Come home with me. I've rye bread and molasses."

"No, Ursula. I need to go home. I need to be alone before I have to report back to the station. I'll call on you," she demanded and whisked east toward Mabyn Square.

I dropped the heavy stack of work at home but quickly left to visit Pype at the soup kitchen. When I arrived at the coliseum, only Gunnar stood behind the narrow table.

"Mr. Gunnar," I called, "where is Pype?"

"I'm not sure," he said and stirred a thick bisque in the metal pot. "He never arrived this morning. I am planning to go check on him when Mr. Tackett stops by to serve for the evening rush."

"I'll go now, Mr. Gunnar. Thank you!" I exclaimed and scurried away.

As I rushed through the square and across Bally's Way toward Pype's apartment, my heart pounded and my mind played horrible images of him ruthlessly stabbing Thaddeus Jessop in Dugald Alley. Pype was probably nursing wounds that he received in the altercation. Or furiously washing the blood stains from his clothes. Or hiding in fear. Or punishing himself for his sin.

"Pype! Are you in there? Pype?" I called loudly as I pounded on the beige door.

"What's this racket?" An elderly man without a hair on his head or a tooth in his mouth threw open his door across the hall and scolded me. "I'm trying to nap!"

"I'm sorry, Sir. Have you seen Pype today?"

"I wouldn't know him if I did see him! Now quit that banging!" he exclaimed.

"Pype," I spoke quietly through the door as my eyes watered, "please answer me."

But he didn't.

I sat on the couch with my knees tucked beneath my chin and Ma's quilt draped across my chilled feet. Garfunkel had left his familiar spot in the windowsill to rest his furry gray and white body against my hip. It was as if he knew how distraught I was. The only other time he'd come to me in such an affectionate way was the dreadful day that Ma left.

I'd sat on that sofa for hours and watched the sky turn from gray to black while tears poured, and I erased them with the back of my hand. Not only did I mourn for my sister who sat heartbroken in the station, I mourned for my relationship with Pype. Ma had promised me that she knew his heart to be good and decent, and although he had rid this world of evil when he stabbed Thaddeus, he was not the man I believed he was. His darkness, which I never knew existed, had come to light.

I did not know how long I'd been sleeping when the quiet knocks on my door woke me. My eyes opened, and I realized the terrible pain in my neck from its awkward position wedged between a throw pillow and the back of the sofa.

"Coming," I called and threw Ma's quilt on top of the sleeping cat before rushing to the door.

I opened it to see Pype at the threshold with a small smile on his tired and unshaven face. Before he could even speak, I grabbed him and pulled him close to me. He wrapped his arms around me and buried his stubbly cheeks into my shoulder.

"What have you done, Pype?" I whispered before pulling away.

"Ursula-" he began.

"Do you realize what you have done?" I shouted and slammed the door. "Not only have you put my sister through terrible heartache, but you've put me through it as well! I know Thad was a despicable person, but-"

"Ursula! Stop! Sit down."

I wiped my glassy eyes and sat next to the poor cat that was still struggling to get from under the quilt.

"Where've you been all day? In hiding? I thought you'd gone back over to the north side or tried to escape to Withe or Swansea or-"

"I've been at the station all day, Ursula." He took my hand into his. "I've been interrogated for hours by some daft fellow with wretched bangs named Caldwell."

"Mr. Inchcape?"

"I did not kill Thad, Ursula. Two squad members arrived on my doorstep early this morning and took me down to the station for questioning, but I did not do it."

I sighed with relief. "Who then?"

"There was a confession. While Caldwell was badgering me right before I came here, someone confessed. She walked right in off the street and declared that she'd done it. She killed Thad last night in Dugald Alley."

"She?!" I screeched impatiently. "Who was it?"

"Your old friend, Mora Sloane."

I gasped and slapped my hand over my mouth. "Mora? You're sure?"

"She gave plenty of gruesome detail. She was in that alley with him last night. She pulled a paring knife on him and diced him like an onion. She brought the weapon with her to the station. It had not yet been cleaned."

I winced at Pype's grisly words.

"I don't understand." I darted my eyes around the room. "She mentioned Thad to me when I saw her in the woods during breakfast that day. She told me to question him about her misfortune. I thought nothing of it really. I just assumed he'd arrested her at some point or that he'd possibly courted her on the side and left her heartbroken, but Thad has been with so many women in the past. He's been so unfaithful to Lolly that it did not even startle me."

"You really thought I'd done it?"

"Pype," I said and squeezed his hand, "terrible scenarios have plagued my thoughts today. I'm sorry I doubted you."

"You do know how messy a killing would be? For a person who abhors lentil stains on his apron, murder would be quite difficult to carry out! Blood is impossible to remove!"

"Pype." I sighed.

"I'm sorry you've worried so today." He comforted me with a smile and took my hand into his. "Now will you help that bloody cat get out of that quilt?"

Pype soon fell asleep on my orange bridgewater-style sofa with his head on my lap and his long legs dangling off the end. I ran my fingers through his hair that had already grown quickly since Mrs. Percival trimmed it not long ago and traced his bristly jaw with my thumb. As I studied him, I was overcome with relief that he was truly the good and noble man that I had always believed he was— that Ma had promised he was.

For the first time since I rested my head on my pillow in my room at the base of Mayor Kinneman's yard when I was an adolescent, I envisioned children. I could see them frolicking in the back yard of a shaded home on Gaius Hill with blueberry juice stains on their lips. They squealed with delight and blew dandelion petals into the wind. They didn't don light eyes and sandy hair like Prentice Fawkes. No, their eyes were dark as coffee and their hair brown and shaggy like the man who slept peacefully on my lap.

FIFTEEN

When I entered the penitentiary on 2nd Street, a small gathering of people loitered in the damp and dim foyer. They conversed quietly around an old man slumped in a wooden chair against the wall.

 I walked to the same hefty guard who was stationed behind his desk when I'd visited Shiloh Pethlen weeks before. Again, he was engulfed in cigarette smoke while he talked quietly into the black phone in front of him. When he finally noticed me standing there, he pulled the receiver away from his ear and revealed his dark teeth through a smile.

 "Here to see Pethlen again, eh?" His large stomach jiggled as he spoke.

 "No Sir." I cleared my throat. "I'm actually here to see the young woman brought in last night. Mora Sloane."

 "You'll have to take a number," he said and nodded to the people in the corner. "She's quite the popular one."

 I turned to examine the small group. Of the four of them standing there with arms crossed and conversing softly, I only recognized Kit Wareham. Her father, Kee, had operated the *South Side Sentry* many years ago– before the north withheld printing ink from us because Mayor Dunbryll claimed the *Sentry* was distributing false news, inciting hate and plotting chaos toward his people. From time to time, though, Kee would dip into his sacred stash of ink, fire up his printing press and pen a story that he believed was of great importance. He wrote when Bally set fire to Front Street, when Tybee Watkins scribbled an alias in the registry and was executed in Algirdis Square, when the mill closed and dozens of men sat on the sidewalks drowning in despair, when northern officials pillaged our crops for their holiday banquet and contaminated our drinking water and now, judging by his daughter's presence at the penitentiary, he planned to run a story on Mora Sloane. I could see the headline: *Missing Girl Returns to Kill Squad Member*

 I took a seat in a chair opposite of Kit and her entourage

and locked eyes with the elderly man drooping in his seat. Beneath that snowy hair and incredibly wrinkled face, I recognized him. It was Ames Sloane, Mora's father. He did not resemble the man who paced the streets night after night looking for his daughter over a decade ago, but it was certainly him. He would not break our stare even when his thin and shriveled lips began to move.

"What's that, Mr. Sloane?" Kit bent down and asked him.

Again the old man mumbled while his eyes still focused on me.

"I can't understand, Mr. Sloane. What's that you say?" Kit repeated.

"Unfortunate Ursula Underwood," he croaked and slowly pointed a crinkly, shaking finger in my direction. "Unfortunate Ursula Underwood!"

The group of people turned to look at my stunned face.

"Unfortunate Ursula Underwood! He went to buy your sister's bed, but the old fool wound up dead! Unfortunate Ursula-"

"That's enough, Mr. Sloane. There, there," Kit shushed him and lowered his trembling finger. "There, there."

I glared at the old man, my heart pounding, and I finally knew where Mora had inherited her malice.

"I think I'd like to see Mr. Pethlen while I wait," I quickly said and walked over to the guard behind the desk.

"What's that all about there?" He nodded to old Ames Sloane drooling from his gums and eyeing me.

"Mr. Pethlen, please, Sir?"

"Yeah, yeah," the guard said and stood before tucking his wrinkled shirt into the back of his pants. "Follow me here."

"Mr. Pethlen?" I called into the dark cell from the ladder-back chair. "It's Ursula Underwood."

"Underwood?" He walked into the dim light and sat on the small stool. "It's right busy here today, innit? Folks have been coming in and out for hours. Young girl was brought in last night I hear. Say she killed a squadron member."

I nodded. "Yes, Sir. I'm here to see her actually. I thought I'd pay you a visit while I wait if that's quite alright?"

"Alright, indeed!" He smiled widely and ran his old fingers through his bushy beard. "What's your business with the girl?"

"She killed my sister's beau last night," I replied very matter-of-factly.

"Oh. Underwood, I'm sorry to hear that." His rugged face saddened.

"Don't apologize, Mr. Pethlen," I answered. "I wasn't quite fond of him. He treated my sister horribly for many years. Of course I would not wish death upon him, but I'd be carrying on if I was to sit here and act terribly devastated about it. That's just the truth of the matter."

"I understand." He nodded. "When the good die, such as your old man, Levon, it's a hard pill to swallow. When the bad are put to rest, the pill goes down a sight easier, yeah?"

"I recently asked my ma if murdering the evil is ever justified. Of course she didn't proclaim that it is, but I was secretly hoping that she would. She's a firm believer in loving the unlovable, but I found it quite hard to love my sister's beau. Oh, I ache at my sister's loss because she truly cared for him, but I cannot say that I will shed many tears at his funeral."

"Your ma possesses much wisdom, Underwood. Have you followed her advice concerning Oden Barmouth? You found it in your heart to pardon him yet?"

"Not yet, but a fellow I've been spending time with is nudging me to speak with Oden. I'm considering it."

"Very well, then, Underwood! Loads that will do for you." He continued to stroke his beard. "And you've been seeing a fellow, eh?"

I nodded. "He's quite decent, Mr. Pethlen. He's the first I've cared for in many years. I feel quite joyful about our courtship."

"Young love is indeed a blessing. Sometimes when I close my eyes, I still see my sweet Bale. If I'd not been overtaken by the evilness of my rage and done what I done when I was a foolish boy, sweet Bale and I would be married to this day. We probably would've had a couple of young ones, and I'd be blessed enough to devour her pulled pork and apple grilled cheese after church on Sunday."

"That's my favorite dish! The diner on 7th serves it up nearly like my Ma's! I should bring you a helping."

"I can taste it now!" He smacked his lips. "When I done what I done, of course Bale had to move on. I heard she married one of the Knighton twins. Not sure which one. Hope it wasn't the short one with the crazy eye."

"I know Mrs. Bale Knighton. She lives on Abermaw in a small A-frame. She keeps canaries. She is married to Deckle. His eyes are right fine."

"Deckle! That's him! Well, I'm glad to hear it wasn't the other one. Fellow looked like an old dog I once had." Shiloh Pethlen crossed his eyes, and our laughter echoed in the murky hallway.

"I wanted to let you know that I found our last meeting quite refreshing." I coughed at the mildew hanging in the air. "All that you said about the war between my spirit and flesh and salt and light made great sense."

"It's an internal struggle we all face, Underwood."

"I've tried not to be so predictable, too, Mr. Pethlen. I'm certainly trying to love the unlovable. I'm trying to follow my spirit instead of my flesh. I'm trying not to analyze so much. I'm trying to find joy."

"It's not an easy assignment, but it's a worthy one."

"Just then, though." I nodded down the hall to the foyer. "An old man out there was right nasty toward me. I would be telling a tale if I said that I didn't want to pounce on the old codger and pelt him square in his nose."

Shiloh laughed. "Well, that'd be quite the sight, wouldn't it, Underwood? I'm certainly enjoying your honesty today. Who is this old codger you speak of?"

"Ames Sloane, Sir," I answered.

"Oh!" He slapped his bony knees. "Well, if any old codger needed pelting, that would be the one!"

"You know him, yeah?"

"I certainly do." He chuckled. "Ames and my older brother, Sidney, went to school together. My brother didn't well tolerate him. They were nemeses and got into several altercations over the years. One time Sidney dumped a bucket of pig manure on old Ames! It's rumored that if you get close enough to him, you can still get a scent of that pig scat! My brother was quite the comic!" Mr. Pethlen fondly remembered his brother before his smile faded. "Sidney crossed over not long after I was put in here– played a joke on the wrong man over the bridge. A northern squad fellow by the name of Colwyn shot him right between the eyes and then made the trip here to tell me all about it. How he laughed when he said my brother was dead." Mr. Pethlen shook his head. "But you know, Underwood, Sidney is with my folks now. They've all crossed over together. That gives me great peace. I've got great peace that I'll be along with them soon, too. Must be a sight better than this dingy hole, innit?"

"Certainly," I said.

"You know, I was hoping you'd pay me another visit, Underwood. I had a dream since your last visit that I've been eager to share with you."

"What's that, Mr. Pethlen?" I leaned forward in the ladder-back chair.

"I believe I told you that my parents sometimes visit me here. In a glorious mist, they appear. They are so present that often times I can even smell my mother. She had such a distinct scent of lavender soap and cleaning powder. I always found great comfort in that smell." His blue eyes glossed over. "But several nights after your last visit, another came to me in a mist. I don't know that I've ever seen her before on the outside. Her skin was like ivory, her eyes were emerald and her hair was glowing, Underwood. Just like the insects that light up the night sky. Glowing, it was! I've never seen a more natural and beautiful shade of gold."

"Did she say anything, Mr. Pethlen?" My voice cracked.

"She thanked me. That's all she did."

"Thanked you, Mr. Pethlen?" I inquired. "Whatever for?"

"She did not say, but I had quite the strong feeling that it concerned you, Underwood. That's why I wanted to share the experience with you."

"I'm-"

"And her scent! It was cleaning powder, similar to my mother's. And maybe I detected a hint of apple." He smiled and paused. "Your ma, Underwood? Was she a maid like my own mother? Scrubbed floors with lavender soap? A great cook, as well? Prepared many an apple and pulled pork grilled cheese for you, yeah?"

I silently nodded while tears streamed from my eyes.

"I feel as if your bond is still quite strong. You speak to her still?"

"I do." I wiped my nose with the sleeve of my wool coat.

"Tell her I don't deserve her thanks, but she deserves mine. Thank her for raising you well, Underwood. I told you on your last call that you've given me a positive glimpse of what remains out there. You've given me conversation. And because I was able to pass a little guidance to you on your last visit here, you gave me a purpose even though it seems impossible for a criminal destined to a dingy cell to have one. So, thank her, Underwood. Thank her for whatever seed she planted within you that made you come to see me."

"I'll do that." I sniffled, quickly nodded and stood from the chair. "Good day, Mr. Pethlen."

"Good day, Underwood."

As I hurried down the dark, damp hallway toward the foyer of the penitentiary, I furiously rubbed the dampness from my face. Then I marched back to the front desk.

"May I see Mora Sloane yet?"

"She's still got visitors. You'll have to wait your turn. Don't think you want to be in the firing line of that old man again, yeah?" he asked.

"No," I said. "I will-"

I was interrupted by the sound of Kit helping decrepit Ames Sloane down another dark hallway at the left of the foyer.

"She's a wretched and ungrateful twit!" Ames mumbled and spit as Kit helped him by the arm. "Wretched and ungrateful! The worry over her nearly put me in the grave! It killed her mother! I'm just a shell of a man now! She tarnished the Sloane name! Wretched and ungrateful twit!"

"There, Mr. Sloane," Kit pacified him as they approached us. Instead of looking to me, he directed his stare at the hefty guard behind the desk and gravelly proclaimed, "Let her fry! I've worried enough over that girl in this lifetime! When she's dead at least I'll know for certain that she isn't roaming the streets or furthermore ruining our name!"

The hefty guard wiped a glob of Ames' spit from his cheek and watched him slowly disappear out the door. He looked to me and said, "Delightful chap, innit? I guess the girl is yours now. Let us go."

We walked down the hallway adjacent from Shiloh Pethlen's block. Instead of bars on the cells, there were large, metal doors with lone windows at the top. We halted at a door near the end of the hallway, and I peered through the smudged glass.

"You've another one!" The hefty guard banged on the door and then left me alone. The cell was dim, just as Shiloh's, and Mora sat on a small cot in the corner. Her blonde hair was pulled tightly into a bun. Her face was pale without makeup.

"Oh, bloody hell." She looked at me. "Unfortunate Ursula Underwood."

"I believe the unfortunate one occupies your side of the door, Mora." I spoke through a small opening beneath the window.

"Back to gloat, I see! Well, gloat away!" She stood and approached the heavy door. "Gloat away! Oh, I know! I know! I know I harassed you when we were mere children and teased your sister and laughed at your heartache! Wasn't I just dreadful to you, Unfortunate? And now here I am!" she proclaimed sarcastically and threw her hands in the air. "Now here I am, sentenced to death. Just gloat away!"

"I haven't come to gloat."

"Then why are you here?" she angrily shouted and put her hands on her slender hips.

"I came to ask why. Why did you kill Thad?"

"Are you heartbroken over it, Unfortunate? I did your sister and you both a favor. It's a favor, innit?"

"I wouldn't-"

"For fifteen years he kept me in that flat! Fifteen years he hid me away from the world! I'd stab him again if I had to! I'd rather sit here in this jail cell and finally cross over than be kept in that ratty flat on 3rd street for another moment!"

"Thad kept you there? All these years?"

"Are you surprised, Unfortunate Ursula Underwood?" She stood directly in front of me on the opposite side of the glass. "You're surprised that he was capable of such cruelty? Certainly not! You are aware of the abuse he bestowed on your sister, yeah?"

"I am." I nodded as Mora began to pace her cell again.

"Oh, he lured me in when I was just a girl. Promised me he had connections in Wheatsand. Said his grandfather grew up near Brannock Castle and was going to send for him one day. He was going to take me there, but we had to stay here just a little longer. It was always just a little longer! That was his empty promise! He put me up in that wretched flat and addicted me to all sorts of concoctions. I wanted to leave but couldn't because I craved it so. He gave me what I needed. Without it, I had such fits and tremors, and he was the only one who could get it for me!" She looked to the floor, ashamed, as she continued to pace.

"Papavar, Mora? He gave you Papavar?"

"Of course he did, stupid Ursula!" She banged on the door. "Put me in a trance, it did. For fifteen years I sat there craving it.

But I finally broke free!"

"The night I saw you limping away?"

"Unfortunate Ursula Underwood, that's surprisingly astute of you, innit?" She laughed cruelly. "Yeah, I'd had enough. So I went to the woods and had fits and nightmares and tremors for days on end. But then it was done. It was out of my body, but I couldn't go home after so long. What could I do?"

"Report it to the squad, Mora. You should have—"

"The squad is in on this whole thing, you twit!" She raced toward me. "They knew Thad was keeping me there! Is it a wonder they never found me at my father's request? Whitchurch and Stevenwill knew. They're probably shaking in their boots that I'll squeal on them. That's why I turned myself in! I'm taking half that squad down with me. They're probably shaking in their boots, yeah!"

I remained silent, stunned.

"And Thad sold me to three northern men." She paced again as my heart began to pound. "Had them come over the bridge and use me every few seasons. Those men paid for me with Papavar. Brought it over in a huge abundance, they did! One man, Garrick, fancied me more than the others. The squad knew all about them, too. Knew they were bringing Papavar over to me, and they looked the other way as a favor to Thad. They're all a wretched lot! All of them! I'm going to tell it all, Unfortunate!" She stopped in front of the window again. "They'll put me to death surely, and I don't suspect Mayor Kinneman will even believe me, but I'm going to tell it all! Fifteen years he kept me there."

"Oh, Mora." I sighed and shook my head. "Lolly didn't know?"

"Nah, she's a daft one, that Lolly. Didn't even know her beau had another woman caged only half a mile from her house. Didn't even know! But I suspect if she did that she'd have stayed with him. At least I was drugged. At least that's what kept me there with Thad. That's my excuse. Your sister was just mad enough to love him."

"I will agree with you there."

"So I've done us all a favor, you see? By killing Thad, I've given your foolish sister her freedom back, and I've obtained my freedom as well. I may not be free in here, but I'll soon cross over. They'll stick a needle in my arm, and I'll be reunited with my ma. I'll finally be at peace from this forsaken place. I'll be the fortunate one and you...you'll still be trapped here. You'll still be Unfortunate Ursula Underwood. That's who you'll always be." She glared at me through the dirty pane.

"Yes." I nodded. " I suppose you've always had an advantage over me."

"Always have," she agreed.

"Unless, of course, you cross into the fiery pit, Mora. Have you thought of that? If you don't sincerely repent for all of your ills while you still have time and ask for grace, I'm certain that's where you'll go. And there's nothing fortunate about that. May the Most High have mercy on your soul."

I watched fear overtake Mora's face before I quickly turned and walked toward the foyer.

"Is that all, girl?" the hefty guard asked from his post. "I've got a traitor in the south block and a lovely fellow who craves the taste of flesh in the north. Want to encourage them while you're here? Innit that your purpose? To encourage these despicable people?"

I shook my head. "I've had my fill of this place today."

SIXTEEN

"My name is Investigator Arundel of the North Side Squadron. I've some questions to ask."

"Certainly." I opened my door wider and let the man clamping long, black lapels inside my home. He immediately made his way to my couch, removed his heavy overcoat and revealed a wine-colored vest over a starched white shirt.

"What business do you have there?" He nodded to the stack of work next to the black typewriter before sitting on my couch.

"I'm employed by Mr. Leo Magnus. I am responsible for data entry."

"Concerning the palladium mine?"

"Yes, Sir. That is correct."

He pulled a notebook from the pocket of his plum vest and began to write.

"May I get you some tea?"

"No," he replied sternly. "Take a seat here please."

I did as he requested and folded my hands on my lap. I curiously eyed the pronounced cleft in his chin.

"You are Ursula Underwood? And this is 22413 Downforge Alley, South Side, Mabyn State?"

"Yes, Sir." I nodded.

"Very well," he said while writing. "Ms. Underwood, it has come to our attention across the bridge that your brother-in-law's murderer, Mora Sloane, is accusing three north side residents of vile behavior. Are you aware of this claim?"

My heart began to pound. "I visited Mora in the penitentiary yesterday, and yes, she mentioned that three men came over the bridge every few seasons to abuse her. They paid Thaddeus Jessop in Papavar for the privilege."

Investigator Arundel wrote. "Did you ever have contact with those three men?"

I gulped. "I did not know the men."

He looked at me for a moment before reaching into the

pocket of the coat thrown over the end of my couch. He pulled out several small tintypes.

"You've never seen these men?"

I quickly scanned the photographs. There was an image of the malicious man in the fedora and one of Garrick, with his thin mustache, posing alongside a beautiful yet far-from-plain wife and four small children. The last tintype was of the nervous white-bearded man with tortoiseshell glasses proudly standing in front of a storefront labeled "Blarney's Housewares."

"No, Sir," I stammered and shoved the photos back at him.

"Ford Binstead, Garrick Norton and Hulbert Blarney were last seen by several northern residents crossing the bridge to the south side, but they never returned."

"Oh," I said.

"With the claims Mora Sloane is making, we are questioning anyone close to the matter. Has your sister Lolly said anything about these three men?"

"No, Sir. My sister was oblivious to anything regarding Mora Sloane. She adamantly refuses to believe that Thad kept Mora in that flat for so many years. She's in shock, Sir."

"Did Mora Sloane admit to harming those men when she spoke to you?"

"No, Sir."

"You must understand that three men do not just vanish. These fellows were pillars in the northern community, Ms. Underwood. Dr. Ford oversaw hospital and acted as Mayor Dunbryll's chief physician! Garrick Norton was a highly decorated school teacher. Hulbert Blarney operated our housewares store."

"Yes, they do sound like very reputable men."

"I've no idea why they would venture south, and I have a hard time believing Mora Sloane's theory, but if they did come here to abuse Mora Sloane and smuggle Papavar then it bears to reason that Mora or Thaddeus had hands in their disappearance."

"Possibly so, but I know nothing of it."

"Why did you go and visit Mora Sloane at the

~ 174 ~

penitentiary?"

"I went to ask her why she murdered Thad."

"You and Mora Sloane are not friends then?"

I laughed. "Sir, far from it! Nemeses would be a more accurate word."

"And over all these years, you had no knowledge of your sister's beau keeping her locked up in a flat on 3rd Street?"

"I had no knowledge of it. I am nearly as shocked as my sister, Sir."

"So you would not be one to help Mora Sloane dispose of these men who she claimed harmed her? As a friend?"

"Sir, I would not."

He studied me closely and leaned forward.

"Do you believe Mora Sloane and Thaddeus Jessop would be capable of harming these men?"

"Mora murdered Thad, Thad nearly killed my sister on many occasions and kept Mora hostage, so of course I do. I believe they were capable of many wicked things. I know they were."

"Sometimes, Underwood, the dead talk. Sometimes they return in a mist or a dream or-"

"Yes, Sir, but if those three men visit you in a mist and confess their killers' name, it will not be mine."

"Very well." He nodded, stood and put his coat back on. "If you receive any information, I trust you will reach out to me?"

"Of course I will, Sir." I saw him out the door.

My spirit grieved at the lies I'd just told. Perhaps I'd saved Mr. Huxley, Chester and Galvan− three good men− from hanging in Algirdis Square, but conviction still poured over me as I watched the investigator descend the stairs of my building. Garfunkel purred and rubbed against my leg as I whispered to the Most High, "Forgive me."

When Pype and I left the diner on Thursday evening, we cut through Dugald Alley.

"This is the first time I've walked this path since Thad was killed," I said as the rats scurried into the shadows. "I will never pass through here without thinking of him again."

"How is Lolly?" Pype squeezed my gloved hand.

"She is finally beginning to accept the truth. She feels so deceived that Thad kept Mora for so many years. Of course she knew of the infidelity. But for him to be callous enough to hold someone in captivity and pump her with mind-altering concoctions is baffling! She's angry with Thad, yet she still mourns him. He was all she's known for so long. Even when the chain is removed, I guess it feels right foreign without it, yeah?"

"I suspect she will soon embrace her new freedom. I deem she'll have a right bright future."

We quietly exited the alley and headed toward Hannelore Park.

"I don't like you venturing here alone, Ursula. You've never gotten in trouble on your trek here on Sunday evenings?" He broke the silence.

"I've had a few scares but nothing too frightening. Men have lurched from the shadows to ask for money or a bite to eat. They have said derogatory things, but most have seen me around here before. They don't know my business here so I'm sure they are curious, but they don't much bother me. "

"You just sit there and watch him?" he asked as we crossed over the railroad tracks and peered across the calm river.

"Yeah."

"And what's the purpose in that?"

"I suppose I take pleasure in seeing him lonely and heartbroken. It's shameful, I know."

"Who was Oden Barmouth before he killed your papa?"

"I am unsure, Pype," I said as we reached his shack. The lamp was lit and there he sat in the middle of the lone room, staring at nothing.

"There." I nodded as we sat on the cinderblock porch across the dirt path from his home. A hunch-backed man limped in front of us, breathing rapidly, but he paid us no mind.

"I find it right pitiable, despite what he's done," Pype said.

"He killed an innocent man, Pype," I replied. "Shot him right in the chest. He murdered a decent man with a pregnant wife and young daughter at home."

"I know that." He squeezed my hand. "And it's a deplorable crime, but to be riddled with that guilt every waking moment? To roam about with no real purpose? Destined to a shanty on the river without family or friends? I cannot help but find pity in that."

"I'm not certain he is sorry for what he's done. Possibly he mourned in the cell across from Pethlen's simply because he'd been caught?"

I ceased speaking when I noticed a group of men emerge from the shadows. They pounded their boots down the dirt path and headed directly toward Oden's home.

"Who is that?" Pype whispered.

"I'm unsure."

"We should go," he said quietly and began to stand.

"No." I tugged on his shirt.

Several of the men walked into Oden's shack without knocking on the unstable door. Those who could not fit inside the shanty stood outside, but they left a view for us through the dingy window panes.

"That's Jemison Alcee," I said over the sound of Jemison's loud but unintelligible voice.

"What does he want with him?"

"I don't know," I answered right before Jemison reared his fist and punched Oden Barmouth in the nose. He and his entourage cheered enthusiastically as Oden slumped from his wooden chair, fell to the floor and disappeared from our sight.

The gang slowly filed out of Oden's small shack. They disappeared down the dirt path and into the shadows of Hannelore

Park.

"We should help him, Ursula," Pype insisted. "Come."

"I cannot," I said. "I cannot face him."

"You can, Ursula. It's time. Let's go." He stood and pulled my hand.

I reluctantly walked behind Pype as we crossed the path and approached Oden Barmouth's home. Through the opened door that barely hung on hinges, we saw him slowly squirming on the dirt floor as blood poured from his nose.

"Mr. Barmouth?"

He startled and looked up at us before shielding his face with his hands.

"Please, I've nothing else to give. Nothing," he pleaded with terror in his voice. Lying there, defenseless, he certainly was not the same callous killer that I had always envisioned.

"I'm here to help, Sir." Pype gently reached down and took his arm. "Allow me to help you to your feet."

Oden looked at Pype, stunned, and slowly steadied himself on worn brown shoes with a large hole on the top of the left toe.

"Have a seat there." Pype lowered him into the chair.

I was standoffish and leaned against the doorway of the shack, my heart palpitating and my eyes fixated on the old man's thin, bony face. His greasy, dark hair was gray around the temples and strands that were usually slicked straight back had fallen into his eyes. He raked his trembling and dirty hand through it and laid it back flat.

"Thank you, Sir," he mumbled.

"Have you any water?" Pype looked around the tiny dirt room.

"I've a bit in a glass jar in that chiller."

Pype walked over to the small tan cooler and pulled a glass jar of muddy water from it. Oden noticed him grimace at the color.

"The Winnow's water isn't what it used to be. Northerners contaminate it on purpose, you know, just so we are forced to purchase a clean lot from them." He took the jar from Pype.

"Thank you."

Pype looked at me and nodded for me to introduce myself to my father's killer. I sternly shook my head and refused. He sighed at me in frustration.

"What did Jemison Alcee want with you, Mr. Barmouth?"

"Ah," he grunted. "Coins. It's always about coins, innit? They're the root of all evil."

"How much do you owe him, Sir? Possibly I could repay your debt if he poses a threat to you?"

"You wouldn't?" He looked up at Pype with disbelief. "Why would you make such an offer? Who are you?" Oden then slowly turned his wrinkled neck toward me. "And who are you? Why are you here? You don't belong in the park. Why are you here? I've seen you here before."

I stammered and shrugged.

"My name is Pype Tyburn, Mr. Barmouth," he paused. "And she is Ursula. Ursula Underwood."

Oden Barmouth turned toward me again, his thin lips parted and his eyebrows raised and forming definite lines on his forehead. The jar of dingy water dropped from his hands and made a thud on the dirt floor, leaking and producing mud.

"We," Pype stuttered, "we happened to be walking through and saw Jemison hit you. We only meant-"

"Levon's girl?" he interrupted Pype and continued to stare wide-eyed at me.

I nodded silently and looked down to my dusty boots.

"I," he stuttered and covered his mouth with his dirty hand. "I should have recognized you. You– you resemble your mother."

I remained silent.

"I've seen you before, but I did not realize who you were. I should have known. You resemble your mother. Yet your hair does not glow. You are a dark-haired replica."

"How do you know my mother's hair glows?" I asked.

"I see her." He removed his hand and slowly grinned. "She's the only comfort I know."

I glanced at Pype.

"She's the only comfort I know in this life." His chin quivered as if he was about to sob. "Your ma, yeah, she's forgiven me of that horrible thing I done."

"I know," I replied softly.

"But you, dear girl, you do not?" He looked up at me from the wobbling chair. "You find me repulsive, yeah? I'm the man who took your pa from you, who left your ma a widow. I'm the man who prohibited your sister from knowing her pa."

I said nothing.

"All I have are these words, but they bear much weight, Ms. Underwood. I am sorry. I truly am sorry for that thing I done."

I blinked to keep my eyes from watering and picked at my fingernails.

"I served much time in that penitentiary, but when I got out, I took my sentence with me. When I got out of that hole, my own parents were long dead." He looked to his shabby shoes. "I was released to nothing. I've nothing. I'm quite alright with that. This is my lot in life. This is my lot for taking your pa's life. I accept that. This is what I deserve."

"You're repentant then?" Pype asked him.

"Every second of my life, I am." He looked over at Pype and then back to me. "I did not mean to take your pa's life. I did not mean to take anyone's life that day at Skett's. All I wanted were some coins to pay a gambling debt. Coins are the root of all evil, yeah? My parents would not let me have the loan. I just needed some extra to put with my wage from the cleaning shop. I worked the steaming press there. I just needed 18 coins. I had not even planned to make the hit on Skett's shop. It was a last minute decision. I wasn't versed well with guns. I did not even know I had shot until your pa went limp on top of me. It was not premeditated. It was-"

"Enough," I quietly interrupted him and held up my hand. "Enough."

He sat silent for a moment and rubbed his dirty hands

together. Pype walked over to me and wrapped his arm around my waist.

"Your ma." Oden Barmouth grinned. "Your ma tells me I'm worthy of forgiveness. She told me that the Most High sent His own son for that very thing I done. She told me my slate could be wiped clean. Crimson stains washed white as snow and all that. I only recently began to believe her, and I've a peace that I cannot truly describe since she's been visiting me. I've a peace that although I'm destined here in this shack by the river, I can finally forgive myself. Better things wait when I cross over because I've been atoned for what I done. A filthy sinner like me has been forgiven. I know it's true because I feel it. I feel it inside, yeah? I know I've been atoned. Washed white as snow."

"I've been urged by my mother to offer you forgiveness—even to show you kindness and provide for your needs because that's the noble thing to do. That's acting in love, as the Most High instructs," I spoke, "but instead, I have relished in your misfortune. I've sat on that cinderblock stoop across the way and gladly watched you sit in this shack, cold and alone. I've harbored much anger toward you for what you took from my family. I've often thought of knocking on your door and giving you what for. I've had to train my mind not to venture to the dark place that says I should come here and slit your throat as you sleep."

Oden quietly nodded.

"And here I am before you now. I'm looking into your apologetic eyes and hearing remorseful words come from your mouth. I know why my mother visits you. She came to you because it's the lost sheep that needs finding. She wanted to help you find the right way. She comes to you because your regret is evident."

"Regret isn't strong enough a word. I-"

"What do you owe Jemison, Mr. Barmouth?" I interrupted him.

"What?"

"What do you owe?" I repeated.

"Twenty-one coins," he mumbled. "More than what cost your pa his life."

"I reached into the pocket of my wool coat and pulled out what I had. Pype also reached into his pocket and added his change with mine. I counted it.

"Twenty-three," I said and stepped forward.

"I oughtn't to dare-" he began.

"Take it, Mr. Barmouth," I demanded as he reached out his grimy hand with dirt-compacted fingernails. I dropped the coins into it with my right hand and held the bottom of his trembling knuckles with my left as tears poured and left clean streaks on his cheeks.

He looked up to me and his croaky voice shook, "How fortunate it must be to have a heart as pure as yours, Ursula Underwood. How very fortunate, indeed."

"I'll bring a jug of clean water to you in the morning, Mr. Barmouth. Good night," I said and exited the doorway as Pype nodded to him and followed.

SEVENTEEN

When I arrived home from Oden Barmouth's the night before, I was too frazzled by the evening's events to sleep. So I worked diligently on the rest of the data entry– well into the dim light of Friday morning. I dropped the stack on Mrs. Inchcape's desk and conversed briefly about my poor sister who sat in her home on Valoria Bend clutching a photograph of Thaddeus and preparing for his memorial that afternoon.

Although a stubborn cloud seemed to hover over the south, the sun was plentiful that Friday afternoon on the north side of the bridge. I sat on the boardwalk and even removed my coat as the rays warmed my shoulders. I'd drawn two caricatures that morning– one of a hefty red-headed boy covered with freckles and another of a pale-faced toddler who sucked on an orange lollipop and squirmed in her mother's lap.

I took the money that I received for the caricatures, bid Dennison and Swann goodbye and instead of walking directly to the grocer, I lugged my heavy pack to the end of the boardwalk. I was alone as I leaned over the wooden railing and watched the cloudy Winnow River flowing beneath me.

Three years ago I lived with Ma in the yellow house at the base of Mayor Kinneman's yard. In my childhood bedroom, I entered accounting figures on the very desk where I'd learned to write my name and sharpened colored pencils to draw my first caricatures. I helped Ma hang laundry on the line, and we invariably ordered supper at the 7th Street Diner every Sunday evening after chapel. We often strolled by Lolly's home on Valoria in hopes to catch a glimpse of her, and Ma dropped coins into the mugs of the homeless in Mabyn Square. We had the best talks on our walks about town.

Ma preached love and kindness back then, as well, but not with such passion. She'd still slip up from time to time and utter a harsh word toward Oden Barmouth or Thaddeus Jessop. She'd complain when her back pain flared. Her humankind often showed, as all of ours does, but mostly, she was meek and gentle in her words.

Although life was splendid with Ma, I decided that I should leave home. I was nearing 30 and felt that I should have something of my own. I should mature and pay rent and prepare my own meals like other adults. I fancied a flat near Finley on Gwinnett, but I chose the one in Downforge Alley because it was only a five minute trek to Ma on Gaius Hill.

Ma gave her blessing, but I suspected that she did not really want me to go, and I wrestled with great guilt in leaving her and our childhood home. That yellow house fell silent. She cooked meals for one. I was gone. Lolly was gone. Papa was gone. The loneliness broke her heart. I sent her away.

I'd always abhorred Oden Barmouth, but I loathed him to a more severe degree when Ma left. If he hadn't killed Papa, she'd have had a reason to stay. She would not have been alone– she would have stayed for Papa. And when Ma went away, I detested Thad much more, as well. If he did not have such a hold over Lolly, she would still be a part of Ma's life. She would call on Ma more than three times a year. Ma would have stayed for more visits with Lolly. Ma would have hung on. She would have found the will to stay if Oden hadn't taken Papa and if Thaddeus hadn't taken Lolly– and if I had not left.

But she did not stay. She left because she was lonely and had no reason to stay. And when she was gone, I thought I would never hear from her again. I grieved greatly. I questioned what I had to stay for, as well.

But the payphone at 77 7th street rang on the first Sunday that I dined there without Mother. Tears of longing dripped onto my sandwich as that phone relentlessly rang. Bronwyn called from behind the counter, "Ursula, please fetch that! It's giving me a right headache!"

My ma's voice on the line was the last I expected to hear. My knees buckled when she spoke, "Hello, dear." My knees buckled, and I nearly plummeted to the checkerboard floor.

Steadying myself against the wall, I could barely hear her voice over the sound of my heart pounding.

"Ma? Ma, is it you? Is it truly you?"

"Yes, dear daughter."

"How, Ma? How are you-"

"Nothing can separate us, Ursula."

"I don't−" I faltered.

"The love in your heart has been noticed here, and I've been allowed to guide you. You have such a great purpose there."

"Guide me to do what, Ma?"

"To do good things, dear. There are so many good things you have been called to do."

"Good things? Good things for whom, Ma? I do not understand."

"So many people need your help, Ursula. So many people would benefit from your kindness, your charity and your love. There is so much good for you to do there."

"This is not real!" I proclaimed and shook my head. "You've gone away! This is not real!"

"This is more real than anything you've ever experienced, dear daughter."

"What is it like there, Ma?"

"I am whole, Ursula. I am where my soul, where all of our souls, always longed to be."

"It's very beautiful, innit?"

"It is indescribable, Ursula. There are no words in our language to paint the proper portrait. There is nothing there to compare it to. Not the sparkling Welshlynn Sea, the sun shining on Brannock Castle, the emerald leaves of West Dellerby Woods in the warm season. Nothing comes close."

"You aren't angry that I sent you there?"

"Sent me here?" I could tell she was smiling. "Nonsense, Ursula. It was my time to come."

"Your broken heart, broken at my absence, did not take you away? Only hours after I left you alone, on my birthday, you left,

Ma! Is that coincidence? Surely you left because you were heartbroken! You had no reason to stay here! You were heartbroken and that's why you left!"

"Dear girl, what fallacy!" Ma exclaimed. "You did not send me here before my time! On the day I was born 50 years ago, I was already destined to be here on this very day. I only wish I had been in this perfectly divine place sooner! Release that guilt, Ursula. There's no need for it!" she paused. "You are chosen, Ursula. You have been chosen to do many good things. I have been permitted to guide you and teach you the wisdom that I have already gained in my short time here."

"Again, Ma, good things for whom?"

"So many names I will give you, Ursula. Alabaster McKinley, Penney Pallathin, Tulsee Bramblewood, Finley Skett, Doreen Flingo, the countless homeless population. Oden Barmouth."

"Oden Barmouth! Ma, I oughtn't to-"

"You will, dear."

"Unthinkable, Ma! I would never-"

"We've so much to do, dear daughter. You have so much love to share."

"Ma, I must ask. Papa? Have you-"

"I cannot divulge details regarding your papa, dear. It is not permissible."

"Yes, Ma."

"I will phone you next Sunday and the Sunday after for as long as I am allowed to do so. I will be there in the diner with you, as I was when we shared our Sunday meal after service."

"Yes, Ma." I cried.

"You're going to do such good things, dear. I love you. Always."

"Always."

Tears streamed down my face as I watched the water rage beneath the boardwalk. How grateful I was to be permitted contact with my mother.

Blessed. Fortunate.

When I entered the grocery on Whishart Avenue, all of the patrons huddled near the wireless behind the cashier's counter. I could barely hear the broadcast over the small speaker so I moved closer and nonchalantly hid myself at the end of an aisle next to stacked cans of pudding.

We ask that all citizens of the northern side not panic but instead extend your prayers to the Most High for rapid healing. Sons Tavish and Shacklee are at his bedside at this moment, along with extended family. He's being made as comfortable as possible and tonic has been administered for discomfort. Again, we ask that you not panic but instead extend your prayers and well wishes to the family as Mayor Dunbryll rests on Rhoslynn Hill.

The crowd dispersed from the wireless and mumbled quietly as they resumed their shopping.

Tavish is a fine fellow. He will serve well.

Quite lenient if you ask me!

Shacklee is who we need!

Rubbish! Shacklee is a daft twit.

Dunbryll lived a long and good life.

Ulcers are quite painful. I've been plagued with them before. Poor chap.

If only Ford were here. He'd have him fixed up. He kept him ticking for quite a long time. Since he's disappeared, Dunbryll's health has certainly declined.

He's been a good mayor. Kept those dirty southerners in check, yeah?

I hear licorice root will soothe the pain. Pity none grows in Mabyn State.

I left Whishart Avenue and trekked the steep incline toward Rhoslynn Hill where two guards in plush purple uniforms were stationed at the heavy iron gate.

"Stop that southerner!" A broad-shouldered guard wildly waved his baton. "What businesses have you here?"

"I request to see Mayor Dunbryll," I croaked.

They glanced at one another and laughed enthusiastically before the tall, thin one said, "That's a right good one!"

I stood firm and continued to stare at them.

"You're not serious?"

"I can help his ulcers. I know where licorice root thrives. It will ease his pain."

They exchanged a curious glance and the tallest one stepped toward me and demanded, "Tell us where."

"I'll tell no one but the mayor himself," I stated as my heart pounded beneath my coat.

"You dare make demands?" the wide guard angrily shouted.

"Yes, I demand to see him," I said, nervous, but hiding it quite well.

"Steady, there, Olsen. I will ring Milo," the thin watchman said.

He walked to a phone stationed on the gate of Rhoslynn Hill. Through the iron slats, I could see Mayor Dunbryll's massive stone home and the smaller, yet extravagant, dwellings of his family and cabinet members surrounding it.

The lanky guard spoke quietly into the phone for what seemed like an eternity while the other one peered at me. I rested my large canvas bag to the cobblestone and rubbed my sore shoulder.

"He'll see her," he said when he returned to us.

"You're not serious? He'll see this dirty southerner based on her false claim to know where licorice root is growing?" the agitated one shrieked. "Licorice is not native-"

"He's quite delirious from pain. He'll see her."

"Come, then." The broad-shouldered one motioned for me to follow him. "Leave that sack of rubbish here."

I followed him up the cobblestone hill, past homes with ivy growing along the north side and short rock walls surrounding the elegantly landscaped gardens. Soon we reached the towering mansion at the center of the hill with a concrete statue of a young Shaw Dunbryll at the entrance.

"The mayor requested her, Sir," he said to another watchman dressed in violet and stationed at the entrance.

"Very well," the man firmly replied and turned to pull the iron lever on the enormous wooden door.

I entered the great foyer and could not help but notice the massive palladium chandelier hanging from the wooden beams above. Many dark, heavy doors lined the entrance hall, but they were all closed. There were no paintings on the walls, and the gray slate floors were not covered with hand-woven rugs from some far-off land. The only thing occupying the bare foyer was the chandelier and a winding iron and wood staircase.

Another guard, also dressed head-to-toe in purple velvet but decorated with a yellow shoulder sash, stood outside the largest wood-carved door with iron hinges at the end of the hallway.

"The mayor has requested her," the one who had escorted me spoke as the older one with the sash nodded and slowly pulled the iron lever. The guard behind me roughly nudged me in the back and pushed me across the threshold.

"Is this her, Milo?" Mayor Dunbryll called from his four-poster bed with a chenille lace canopy located in the center of the large and elegantly-decorated room.

I immediately recognized Tavish and Pype's kind-looking sister dressed in a graceful rosy gown at the mayor's bedside. At the foot of the bed sat a sour-looking man with long, flowing brown hair and beady eyes. I was certain he was Shacklee.

"Yes, Mayor. She claims to know where licorice root grows," Milo answered.

"Come here, girl." The mayor leaned onto his elbows in the plush bed with stark white sheets.

I reluctantly walked toward him, my heart pounding in my throat.

"What are you called?"

"Ursula Underwood, Sir," I replied and looked at Tavish and Tegwen to see if they possibly recognized my name from Pype's letters. I was unsure by their expressionless faces.

"You claim to know where licorice root grows, eh? In this climate? That is absurd!" He mocked.

"Yes, Sir, I do know."

"Well tell then!" the frightening mayor with yellow teeth and patchy white hair demanded. "Enough of this falderal!"

"I give it to my friend who is also plagued with ulcers. It is a pain reliever. Licorice soothes irritation and reduces inflammation."

"I've Glabra tablets for my ulcers!"

"Yes, Sir, but the licorice in combination with Glabra will expedite healing. Together they will cure you."

"Enough of this runaround! Where is the root, girl?" Shacklee called from the round tufted ottoman.

"I've a request first, Sir." I anxiously shifted my eyes from Shacklee to the mayor.

"What's that?" Mayor Dunbryll barked. "A dirty southerner has dared come here with a request? Shacklee, have my ears deceived me? Am I so delirious from the discomfort that my ears are being affected?"

"Enough of this!" Shacklee snarled. "Do away with her, Milo! She's wasting our precious time!"

"No," Tavish interrupted. "This girl is willing to help. Let us hear what she has to say."

"Lenient, you are, Tavish! Entirely too lenient!" Shacklee criticized.

"Very well, girl! My eldest wants to hear your request. So be it." The mayor winced at the discomfort and fell from his elbows and onto his lush pillow.

"I would like to request the Glabra tablets for my friend who also suffers with ulcers on the south side. He needs something to cure them− not merely ease the pain."

"Fine, fine," Mayor Dunbryll grumbled and casually waved his hand.

"And-"

"There is more?" Shacklee growled and rose to his feet. "Who do you think you are, demanding things from Shaw Dunbryll? How dare you−"

"Shacklee," Tavish pacified him. "Calm yourself. Let her speak."

"My friend's father, the same friend with the ulcer, requires Adamantyl for his tremors. Our physician on the south side refuses to obtain the tablets."

"Adamantyl and Glabra. What else do you require for more ailing southern friends?" Mayor Dunbryll gritted his teeth.

"Nothing, Sir," I said. "Although-"

"I've heard quite enough!" Shacklee furiously paced the

large, elegant room. "I've mind to take her life right here."

"Proceed." Tavish ignored Shacklee and nodded at me.

"I-I would very much like to have a ghost orchid bouquet from one of your heated greenhouses for my brother-in-law's memorial service which will take place later today. They are my sister's favorite. I believe they would bring her some comfort."

"Where is the root, girl?" Mayor Dunbryll groaned in pain.

"You'll honor your promise? I will receive the medications that I have requested, Sir?" I nervously squeaked.

"I'm feeling generous today, so you'll get your tablets! But tell me where the root is before I change my mind and have you executed right here at the foot of my bed! I don't know how many more southern killings I will be privileged to witness. It would suit me just fine to do away with you right now. In fact, it would bring me great joy and take my mind off the pain!" He screamed.

"It's in the deep valley of West Dellerby Woods— near the patch of Heckalia plants."

"Milo!" Mayor Dunbryll called to his guard. "Send one of your men to the location she's just given. Once he's confirmed the root is there, give this girl the tablets that she has requested and a bouquet of orchids," he paused. "Then record her name in the Book of Banished in Algirdis Square. She's never to cross the bridge again. And if she dares request one more thing, have her killed."

I wrapped my arm around a sobbing Lolly's shoulders as gray clouds hovered in the sky and sent a fresh chill through the air. Surrounded by squad members, we stood on the knoll of the cemetery beneath the barren branches of a massive Runyon tree. At the center of our huddle was the copper-colored casket with the Mabyn State symbol adorning the lid. Bouquets of wild flowers and weeds, most unsightly and retrieved from the woods, were placed next to the coffin. Standing out was the Ghost Orchid bouquet that I'd retrieved. Everyone gawked at in amazement and wonder.

Feeble Vicar Fernhill steadied himself at the head of the casket and performed the standard ceremony. He said kind words about Thaddeus Jessop and painted him as loyal friend and dedicated squadron member. I refrained from retching at the dishonesty. The vicar had said the same kind things about my father when he was put to rest nearly 30 years ago. Only then, the reverend was not lying.

Each squad member, including Whishart and Stevenwill, hummed the squad song while they reached down and grabbed a handful of dirt to toss on top of the coffin. I warily eyed the patrolmen and replayed Mora's nasty accusations about them in my mind. I had never trusted Mora Sloane, but I had a feeling that she was being entirely truthful about the spiteful-looking men. I didn't doubt for a moment that they had known she was being held captive for so many years.

Thaddeus' ailing mother, Lark, could barely stand back up once she'd bent over to clutch her handful of dirt. Her nursemaid helped her wobble on crooked legs to the casket, and she showed little emotion when she tossed the cold earth on the state seal. And then Lolly grabbed a mound of soil and pitched it on the top before whispering, "Life is long and my love has gone away from me." She wiped her hands on a coral lace handkerchief before turning and descending the hill.

EIGHTEEN

"Good things this week?"

"Thad is gone, Ma. He's crossed over."

She said nothing.

"I don't mean that's the good thing, but that's the first thing you should know."

"Lolly?" Her voice was saddened. "Is she mourning deeply?"

"Yes, Ma. She is."

"How did he meet his demise?"

"At the hand of Mora Sloane, Ma."

Silence again.

"Thad held Mora captive since her disappearance 15 years ago. He had her hooked on Papavar and confined to a flat on-"

"This grieves my spirit, Ursula. I do not want to know."

"Yes, Ma," I paused. "Do you ever visit Lolly? Do you appear to her?"

"I do not."

"Why is that?"

"I can only appear to those whose hearts are receiving, dear. I can only appear to those who have soft and repentant hearts. Your sister's heart is like stone. She harbors so much anger and resentment. Perhaps now that Thaddeus is gone, she will become receptive— more loving. More like you."

"Oden Barmouth has a receiving heart, then, yeah? He was worthy of your appearance?"

"Ursula," she paused, "you know I've visited him?"

"Pype and I went to see him."

"Dear!" she exclaimed excitedly. "I knew the time would come!"

"He described your glowing hair. Why didn't you tell me, Ma? Why didn't you tell me that you were comforting him? Why didn't you simply tell me that he was remorseful?"

"You had to make the decision to see him on your own, Ursula. I did not want to influence that. It was your choice to make."

"And you've been to see Shiloh Pethlen as well?"

"You've discovered much this week."

"Yes," I said.

"I wanted to thank him, Ursula. I wanted to thank him for the peace he gave you— for the things he told you and the wisdom he shared."

"He desires that I thank you, Ma, for the wisdom you passed on to me."

"Shiloh Pethlen is a dear man. As is Oden Barmouth," Ma paused. "My intentions over the last three years were to show you that the unlovable can be loved, Ursula. People can change. People make grisly choices, but if they are worthy of the Most High's grace, then they are certainly worthy of ours. They are deserving of the same kindness and generosity that you bestow on the widow and the orphan."

"I do see that now, Ma. I truly do understand. A spirit of unforgiveness complicates and compromises our daily walk with the Most High. Forgiving others releases us from anger and allows us to receive the healing we need."

"Ah, you've done well. I am incredibly proud of you."

"I went to Rhoslynn Hill and saw Mayor Dunbryll. He's plagued with ulcers. I bargained with him and told him where licorice grows in exchange for tablets for Finley and his father. I also asked for a Ghost Orchid bouquet for Thad's memorial service."

"Ursula! What a beautiful thing you've done! I foresee that your good deed will have quite an impact!"

"I'm not so sure if it was the wise choice. Dunbryll complied, but then I was forced to sign the banished registry. How will I obtain food or make a wage with caricatures now?"

Ma said, "You are capable of growing your own food and providing for yourself. I would not recommend any gardening advice from Mr. Kestral, however."

I snickered.

"Do not abandon your drawing, either. It's such a cathartic thing for you to pursue. The pleasure you find in sketching is worth more than the coins."

"But what can I do? I would never dare ask a friend to buy goods for me on the north side and risk execution. I suppose Mr. Lisbon would allow me some space to plant in his garden. I suppose I could mend my own clothes and make do without the extra caricature money. Possibly Bronwyn would allow me to purchase blackcurrant tea in bulk from the diner! Oh, how I cannot do without my tea! I have been spoiled by venturing over the bridge. I did not realize just what a service it was to be allowed on the north side even if only a couple of hours at a time."

"When you moved to Downforge Alley three years ago on your birthday, Ursula, you claimed that you wanted independence. You wanted to mature, yeah? Now is the time to truly do that."

"Yes, Ma."

"I'm concerned with your sister and her suffering."

"I would love nothing more than her to stay with me now. I'd be obliged to take care of her until she's stable enough to make a wage."

"You're kind, Ursula, but now is the time for Lolly to learn to live on her own. It's time for your independence to flourish—

and hers."

"She will-"

I was interrupted by Chester barging through the diner's glass doors. Galvan panted and rushed in behind him with his dusty hat in his hand.

"He's dead!" Chester shouted throughout the building as Bronwyn and I looked to him. Tabb emerged from the swinging kitchen doors, and even Hamill Cooper lifted his hung-over head from the table.

"Dunbryll is dead!" He shouted again, both with excitement and dread in his tone.

"Ma," I spoke into the phone as my heart pounded. "Did you overhear? Dunbryll is dead."

She replied quietly, "And with him, his terrifying reign."

I rushed to Pype's apartment when I left the diner to inform him of Dunbryll's passing. He fixed me a cup of blackcurrant tea, and we sat together on the couch. He pulled a letter that he'd received the week before from his bureau drawer and read it to me as smoke circled his head from his before-bed cigar.

Dearest Brother,

I hope all continues to go well for you on the southern side. We still miss you very much. Each time we glance at the empty chair at Ma and Pa's Sunday dinner table, we are overcome with sadness and longing for your voice, your embrace and your tall tales. Aiko continues to brood and diligently watch out the front window for you to walk up the stoop. He's getting on in years, Pype. Thirteen now, which as you know, is an incredibly long time for a Labrador to thrive. He's grayed around his temples and takes a lengthy time to rise to his legs. I wish you could see him again before his time comes. What a faithful friend he was to you.

Ma has become weaker since my last letter. Her physician is a right twit, I believe, and has only advised her to consume iron. He does not know the underlying cause of her feebleness, but like Aiko, she is slow to rise. Pa just watches her with worry.

Glennis has met a boy from Wheatsand. He's rather snobbish, even for me. His father is on the council there, and his mother is dear friends with Lady Abertha. He does not work but rather was born with a silver spoon in his mouth, and Glennis absolutely relishes in it. She's so concerned with hierarchy and prominence. She has certainly changed and is no longer the meek and humble child that you left. Lord, Pype, tell me I'm not that way. Tell me I did not become arrogant when Tavish showed affection for me. It makes my skin crawl to think of it.

Glennis has even changed her views concerning the very people that you felt led to help. No doubt her beau has placed false ideas in her head. And, I feel, she thinks differently of you for going there to aid them.

Tavish's stance is also concerning to me. With Shaw falling ill with ulcers, among other ailments, Tavish opts to spend all of his time at his father's bedside. They are making preparations for Shaw's passing. Tavish is making promises that I never thought he would make, Pype. Possibly he is simply vulnerable as his father slips away. He will not converse with me about it in great detail, but he feels he should carry out his father's dying wishes. There is talk of burning the bridge, Pype. We'd have no contact whatsoever. I know southerners are self-reliant and able to survive with gardening (if northerners do not plunder the crops), but my main concern would be medicines. Possibly you should make plans to acquire as much medicine as you can while you are still allowed north? Possibly get your southern physician on board to obtain scripts? I will smuggle you what I can.

Another discussion on the table is to sever all electricity on the south side. Shaw has threatened to do that for many years, as you know, but the profits he makes on southern electricity has kept him from actually doing so. I believe he's serious this time, though, and is no longer concerned with the small revenue. He told Tavish that he would die a happy man knowing that his enemies were left in the dark.

I do not know how much longer he has. He does seem to have better days than others. Not only are the ulcers plaguing him, but the physician that he's summoned from Wheatsand since Ford's disappearance believes he, too, has anemia and a weak heart.

I know that my husband is a loving, kind man. You know that as well. Tavish and I have had many discussions about the oppression of the southern people, and he has disagreed with his father's malice for many years. But, Pype, he feels a certain duty to his father and the cabinet. Of course Shacklee is filling his head with ideas.

Whatever does happen, Pype, please do not bear a grudge with me. You are my brother, and I continue to love and miss you dearly. Whatever Tavish decides, Pype, please remember that he cares for you, as well, but he is trying to discern where his loyalties lie. So many people expect certain things from him when he becomes heir. Keep him in your prayers.

I wish nothing more than Tavish to lift the ban so you can resume your seat at Sunday dinner. He knows my plea. I'm praying that my desire is more important to him than his father's.

Always thinking of you.

Your loving sister,
Tegwen

Southerners woke on Monday morning to a copy of the *South Side Sentry* on their stoops. The headline DUNBRYLL DIES was printed in faded, sparse ink. People convened on the corners and in the diner to quietly murmur and speculate about the news. What would his death mean for us? How would Tavish rule?

On Thursday afternoon, as Shaw's casket was lowered into the plot on Rhoslynn Hill, cannons fired on the northern side. I was typing figures at the time they sounded throughout the city and shook the window panes. Garfunkel was startled by the boom and leapt into my lap while purring nervously.

"There, there, cat," I said and ran my fingers through his gray and white fur.

I rolled my desk chair across the parquet floor and peered out the window. A scarce crowd of southerners looked toward the north, and they appeared to be nearly as nervous as the cat in my lap. Dunbryll was in the ground. The man who had ordered oppression against us for so many years was buried in the soil. Where he was now was not for me to judge, but I could estimate that his hair was not glowing.

NINETEEN

While inputting data on Friday morning, I suddenly heard commotion outside. I walked over to the window with my cup of blackcurrant tea to see North Side Squadron members, dressed in their flashy purple uniforms, scurrying down the streets while yelling and wildly waving their arms. Children, in single-file, marched from the schoolhouse on Gaius Hill in their hand-me-down navy and gold plaid uniforms. They passed in front of my apartment, and the schoolteachers streamed alongside them. They attempted to comfort the frightened children with soothing glances and nods, although their own fear was apparent.

The purple-clad soldiers barked orders and ushered crowds of the townspeople down the narrow alley, including Mayor Kinneman with his stark white hair and long, gleaming goatee. The apprehension on his face made my head dizzy and my heart palpitate.

I began to pace my apartment, and Garfunkel nervously took every step I did. I gnawed on my fingernails and darted back and forth from the window to observe what was happening. Guards entered the door of my building below, and then I heard the sound of boots barreling up the stairway. There was rapid banging on my door followed by more stomping and then hammering on Ms. Finglo's door down the hall.

"North Side Squad! Open up!" the harsh voices on the other side of the entry demanded. "Open up or we'll break it down!"

I timidly scampered to turn the doorknob and saw two purple guards pacing the hallway between my apartment and Ms. Finglo's. I could not speak before a muscular soldier with sandy hair told me, "Convene in Mabyn Square at once!"

I nodded quietly, slipped into my shoes and retrieved my coat from the hook. Then I turned to look at Garfunkel for possibly the last time.

On the rushed walk to Mabyn, I saw many familiar, yet terrified, faces. Ms. Purvis was shoved down Gwinnett by a scrawny soldier, and another screamed at Barton Huxley to make haste. Crying children clung to their parent's hips, the elderly walked faster than they had in years, and the homeless moved with genuine purpose and direction.

Penney Pallathin, wearing my former sage coat, rushed to my side. Her chestnut-colored hair draped over her distraught hazel eyes. "Ursula, what is happening?"

"I'm unsure." I cautiously darted my stare around the congested street.

"Are they going to execute us all?" Penney nearly cried.

I said nothing and kept walking with my head down.

I searched for Pype in the packed square. I saw the dark man who wore the tall hat and occasionally served alongside Pype, but I could not make my way through the crowd to speak to him. Every member of the southern squad stood to the left of the square— not as cohorts of the northern guards— but also as lowly southerners who had been demanded to trek there. Their faces donned looks of confusion, just as those they were purposed to serve and protect.

"Ursula?" I heard an old, familiar and soft voice behind me. I turned to see Prentice Fawkes. He removed the black flat cap from his sandy mane and revolved it in his hands.

"P-Prentice," I stammered in shock.

"Have you any idea what is happening?" he asked me quietly.

"N-No." I shook my head and gazed at him. This was the first time we had spoken since our school days.

"Your ma has not told you?" He shifted his crystal-blue eyes to a husky guard about 30 yards away from us.

"My ma?"

"I know she speaks to you." He nodded. "Mrs. Geraldine came to me once in a dream. She said that you converse."

Ma had revealed to me that she was only allowed to visit those with receptive, loving hearts. I did not know Prentice Fawkes possessed one of those.

"No, Prentice," I said. "She has said nothing. She cannot foresee the future. She hasn't the authority to do that."

"She said you're doing good things, Ursula. I was not surprised to hear it." His chubby cheeks grinned as I remained silent. "You've always radiated compassion. You've always had a tender heart, yeah? Although school age folly so many years ago, I want to apologize for whatever hurt I caused. For what it's worth, yeah? We may all soon be dead, and I just wanted you to know that." Prentice's voice trailed off…embarrassed.

I smiled at him and nodded as the wind blew my dark hair across my milky face. "Thank you, Prentice."

He returned the flat cap to his head, smiled and disappeared into the crowd.

The hundreds of southern residents silently huddled in the wintry wind while the northern guards maliciously watched us with cold stares. Finally there was commotion at the western entry of Mabyn Square, and the crowd parted. I stood on the tips of my toes, yet I could not quite see what was happening. A hush fell over the murmuring crowd when Tavish Dunbryll ascended the cracked concrete steps and stood at the base of the statue of Dessick Mabyn. Two violet-dressed squad members followed and stood on either side of him. He observed the mass of people for a moment before placing a silver speaking-trumpet to his mouth.

"Southern citizens of Mabyn State," he declared through the trumpet as the fur collar of his long blonde coat blew in the harsh wind. "As you know, my father, Shaw Dunbryll has been laid to rest. On his death bed, he made clear what he requested of me as his heir."

The crowd began to murmur while the purple-clad police shoved around and demanded silence. I furiously scanned the mob of people for Pype. I wanted him next to me. I wanted to lock arms with him and bear the news together.

When all became quiet and only the sound of the gust roaring through the faulty coliseum behind Tavish Dunbryll could be heard, he said, "My father desired for many years to see you left in the dark. He ceased to remove you from the grid only because he made profit on your electricity payment. I've recently learned that the revenue from your power funded the northern side's yearly Orchid Festival. I see no reason why funds cannot be pulled elsewhere to supply this entertainment."

"He's going to leave us in the dark!" a male voice shouted from the multitude. The people murmured again, and the northern squad began to move through the crowd.

"He also desired to destroy the Nairn Bridge. The sole reason the bridge has been left intact for so long is the revenue received from your purchases on the north side."

"We're going to be deserted here!" another terrified voice called, followed by fearful murmuring from the assembly.

"Settle down!" Tavish raised his hand as he spoke into the trumpet. When we were finally quiet, you could almost hear the sounds of our hearts pounding. Tavish looked down to his feet and then raised his head before speaking again, "All of my life, I've been raised to believe that you are a worthless people. I've been taught to abhor you and even to fear you. I've been told nightmarish stories of rebels one day filing over the bridge to slit our throats as we sleep. You've been painted as a sad and desperate multitude that covets life on the north side— a multitude who will eventually rise up and take our women, slaughter our children and control our mine. The last words my father said to me reiterated that. He made it quite clear what he expects of my rule."

No one shouted from the crowd. Instead, tears began to silently fall and fathers pulled their families close to their sides.

"This great man," he paused and pointed to the statue behind him, "did not intend for his state to be ruled this way. Dessick Mabyn lived here on the south side in a beautiful sprawling home where an abandoned steel mill now sits. This, right where I stand, was his favored place in Mabyn State. I intend to make this a favored place again," he said as even the guards who stood behind him and decked in purple looked puzzled. "Because your power and energy payments will no longer be required to fund the festival, I propose lowering your fee. Your electricity costs will instead be used to repair the Nairn Bridge. With my father's body, so died his rule."

Shocked expressions and dropped jaws spread across the gathering. The northern guards conversed with one another and the two standing on the statue with Tavish leaned in to speak with him. Tavish nodded at their words and then held up his hand for them to cease speaking.

"Southern residents, we are no longer two separate entities!" he announced. "You will no longer be an oppressed people. You will no longer be kept at bay out of prejudice and fear. You will be embraced by the north, and you will live as Dessick Mabyn intended for you to live!"

Slowly a roar erupted. Cheers of jubilation echoed throughout the square, and my neighbors jumped up and down and raised fists in the air. I laughed through my tears.

"Mayor Kinneman, will you join me here, please?" Tavish called loudly through the trumpet. Soon the pale, aging man with snowy hair joined him at the base of the statue.

"In unity, we will restore Dessick Mabyn's vision. Hail Mabyn State!" Dunbryll and Kinneman raised joined hands as Mabyn Square erupted once again, and we chanted in unison, "Hail Mabyn State!"

"Ursula!" I somehow heard him call my name over the shouting. I turned to see him only seconds before he lifted me off the ground.

"Pype!" I cried and pulled away to look at his face. "This is true, yeah? This is real?"

"It is, Ursula." He took my face into his hands and kissed me.

"Attention!" Tavish called to the crowd. "Where is my brother-in-law, Pype Tyburn? Will you come forward?"

Pype looked at me, stunned, as I nodded for him to go.

"Bring your friend, Ursula. Ursula Underwood, will you join him, please?" Tavish requested into the trumpet.

Pype looked back at me, grabbed my hand and pulled me through the crowd as I felt pats on my shoulders. We soon stepped onto the large platform beneath Dessick Mabyn. Tavish greeted Pype with a lengthy hug.

"This man," Tavish said while draping one arm around Pype's shoulders, "deserves much praise. You see, he influenced my decision to restore peace. His love and compassion for you people helped me to see that southerners are worthy of our help. You are worthy of what we can provide. And his friend, Ursula—" He looked to me "—this kind woman, this kind *southern* woman, aided my father on his death bed. She aided the man who made her life, all of your lives, miserable for decades." The southerners looked to one another and mumbled. "The kindness in Ursula's gesture boggled my mind because I realized you are not the savages that my father raised me to believe you were. Ursula," he said and looked to me again, "you opened my eyes and cultivated the seed that my brother-in-law planted within me when he came across the bridge to serve. Good people live here. I know that now."

I nodded and wiped the tears from my dark eyes as the southerners looked upon Pype and me with adoration and rapidly clapped their hands.

TWENTY

Spring– when the whole world comes alive. Birds call from trees that are no longer bare. Dandelion petals blow on the warm breeze, and even cloudy, rainy days are welcomed to nurture the new growth. Colors abound, and the sweet scents of blossoms fill the air. A world that recently seemed so harsh and cold becomes welcoming and warm once again. With that warmth, spring also brings hope and rejuvenation for our own lives. Spring is the rebirth. It's when the Most High does new things– new things *spring* forth.

As I walked to the diner on Sunday evening, my wool coat long hidden in the wardrobe and replaced only with a light peach cardigan, the sun hung in the western sky– only by a thread– as if it was not yet ready to retire on such a lovely day. It painted the heavens a pale hue of purple with streaks of orange and pink.

I stopped to peer into the window of Ms. Purvis' shop and saw Barton Huxley sliding a large wooden spatula topped with a browned loaf from the brick oven. Ms. Purvis stood next to him and kneaded dough while they laughed heartily.

It had been a blessing to witness the innocent and much-needed companionship blossom between them. Mr. Huxley delivered bread for her on both the northern and southern sides of the river, and with his wage, he was able to afford the flat below mine. His tattered cardboard sign was displayed on his mantle as a reminder of saving grace, and his burgundy mug caught the change in his pocket at the end of the work day. His worn polyester suit had been discarded, and Papa's boots had been returned to my wardrobe.

"How's the old chap fancy baking bread?"

"Oh, Mr. Barmouth!" I looked away from the window. "You startled me!"

"I'm sorry, Ursula." He grinned as the warm breeze blew

his clean hair upward.

"He fancies it quite well. He has been practicing baking at home, and our entire building smells heavenly. My mouth seems to water all of the time." I smiled.

"The scent of warm bread will do that, eh?"

"And how are you, Mr. Barmouth?"

"Ursula, I wish you would call me Oden. With our history, formalities aren't necessary."

"Very well, Oden. How are you?"

"I'm doing quite well." He nodded. "With the grant received from the northern side to bring structures up to code, I've been commissioned to repair shanties on the river. The strongest gale couldn't knock them down now."

"You're making old things new, Oden."

"Old things have passed away, and new things have come." He smoothed his hair. "I'll be on my way then. I'm trekking over the bridge for several bags of cement. My neighbor, Mrs. Ginerva, has lived far too long on dirt."

"Good day," I said as he walked away.

The diner was bustling with patrons from both sides of the Winnow. They were there to feast on the new Sunday night special of sausage and speckled bread with a side of amber pudding. Northern food critic, Freeman Fritz, had described it in his newspaper column as, "*Absolutely delightful. With each succulent and savory bite, I was taken back to my childhood in Ma-Ma's cottage by the sea.*" I'd yet to try it, though. I still fancied my familiar pulled pork and apple grilled cheese.

Naviana, a young waitress with auburn curls, hustled through the crowd with a serving tray raised above her head. As I walked toward my table in the corner, Bronwyn gave me a quick wave from behind the busy counter before calling to Tabb and his assistant cooks that I had arrived.

I slid into the booth covered with new apple-red vinyl and nodded and smiled at the young couple sitting adjacent from me.

Their bubbly blonde toddler girl squirmed in her father's lap as he attempted to take bites of the sausage. I played a game of peek-a-boo with her as she chortled with glee. The father appreciated my gesture to occupy her so he could eat, and both he and the mother smiled at me genuinely.

"She's right sweet," I called to them.

"Handful, she is," the mother replied and reached across the table to wipe amber pudding from the girl's chubby chin.

"Is this your first time at the diner?" I inquired.

"We've been here several times," said the father. "We're renovating a house on Valoria. We hope to be settled in a few weeks and suspect we'll be regulars here. The food is quite delicious."

"Valoria?" I asked. "Possibly the green wooden house in the bend?"

"You know it?" The woman turned to me in her chair.

"Yes," I said. "My sister lived there for many years."

"We do love it," she replied. "The most beautiful Runyon trees shade the backyard, yeah? I fell in love with them. Our home on the north side doesn't have such beautiful wooded scenery. I can hardly wait to put a swing out there for our Bella."

"I'm pleased to know happy memories will be made in that home," I said. "Happy memories there are long overdue."

I pulled the thin cardigan tightly to my shoulders as the air conditioning roared, and Bronwyn approached my table with the steaming cup of tea.

"Good crowd, innit?" I asked her and took the cup from her hands.

"Certainly is." She smiled. "Will it be just you this evening? Pype?"

"He's working late into the evening. I'll have the usual."

"Won't you try the sausage, Ursula?" Bronwyn pleaded and exposed lipstick stains on her front teeth. "A change may do you some good! Didn't you read Freeman's review in the *Sentry*? It's succulent *and* savory!"

"That's fine and well, Bronwyn, and I'm sure it's delightful, but I'll take the usual. Sausage may conjure many happy childhood memories for Mr. Freeman, but pulled pork serves that purpose for me."

"Well, I cannot argue that."

"And don't forget the carryout order for Mr. Pethlen! He, too, fancies pulled pork and the memories it invokes," I said as the phone rang.

"Happy birthday, dear."

"Thank you, Ma."

"On this day three decades and three years ago, my most beautiful blessing was born— with hair like cocoa and skin like ivory. I was scared to death, Ursula. I hadn't a clue what to do with you! Oh, how silly I looked trying to pin a diaper! I was terrified I would be a right twit at parenting, but you made it easy, Ursula. You were easy to care for, easy to love, and you continue to bless me in ways that you do not even comprehend."

"Ma," I responded as my face blushed warm.

"Please tell me this day no longer bears sadness for you, dear daughter."

"I abandoned you on this date three years ago. Within hours of moving into my apartment on Downforge Alley on my 30th birthday, you were gone. Physician Tryce could not save you. Of course this date bears sadness."

"But am I really gone?"

"It is not the same. You must know that."

"How many times must I tell you that I did not leave because I felt you abandoned me? Your moving from home did not break my heart, dear. I knew that you must leave the nest. I did not perish of a broken heart, Ursula. You should rejoice! I am so thankful to have crossed over. I've no pain or sorrow. I've been reunited with many loved ones that I've mourned for decades. My soul is at home. That should give you great peace."

"It does, Ma," I said. "Of course it does, but I will forever long for you… I covet your hands, Ma. I covet the sight of them, your nails painted peach. I covet them taking me into an embrace and stroking my hair as I rested my head in your lap. I long to see your comforting eyes and gentle smile, and I covet our conversations that lasted well into the night. I miss our dances around the kitchen table and our laughter. I even crave your scent, Ma. I am so incredibly thankful to still be allowed to converse with you like this, but I long for your physical presence. I know that I forever will."

"Dear, sweet daughter," she said, "I long to hold you in my arms, as well, but I would not leave here even if I were given the chance. Doesn't that prove to you how marvelous it is here? Our souls begin here, and here is where they so desire to return."

I silently nodded.

"You do know we will be reunited again— and that it will be forever, Ursula. Eternity, my darling daughter. We will spend eternity together here in glory. We will never be torn from one another again. No more tears or sorrow."

"I cannot wait."

"You will, though, Ursula, because you still have so much to live for there."

I nodded.

"Now tell me of Pype. How is he?"

"Oh, Ma. His beloved Aiko died on Thursday. He shed buckets of tears for that Labrador," I said. "I think that dog could finally let go once they were reunited. I think that old dog died with a happy heart."

"The companionship of an animal is an invaluable thing. I believe you can attest to that with Garfunkel, yeah? That old cat has served you well," Ma said. "What of Pype's parents? Is his mother growing stronger?"

"We dined there for lunch after chapel today. She prepared an elaborate meal with no help from Tegwen or me. She insisted that she do it on her own, and a mighty fine job she did! As Pype's father watched her jovially serve us, I could see quite the burden had been lifted. Pype's presence has helped heal her. I just know it."

"Although Glennis still agrees with her beau's prejudice, I am delighted to know the rest of his family has accepted you as one of their own, Ursula. I know you will bring them much joy."

"They are quite the lovely family."

"And how is Pype's job coming along? He's still serving in the Reconciliation Cabinet?"

"They are making great strides with many northerners. Many who opposed Tavish's rule no longer wanted to be a part of Mabyn State, and they voluntarily seceded to Hebrides or Withe. But, Ma, I hear they are treated poorly there. They are treated similar to the way northerners treated us. Mabyn State refugees are looked down on. I am certain many of them regret the decision to secede. So those who remain and are cross with the reinstatement just glare at us when we pass them on the streets, but they do not stir up much trouble. They know it is better for them here than Hebrides or Withe. They don't have to be friendly with us I guess?"

"No, they do not."

"Lady Abertha has met with Tavish and Mayor Kinneman several times over the months. Although we haven't officially been invited to come and go from Wheatsand, and residents such as Glennis and her beau are adamant in their bias, their meetings have been cordial. It has been made clear that we are no longer adversaries. I do wonder, though, how our cousins feel about the merge. I have such a strong desire to reach out to them, Ma."

"Possibly their hearts are not ready. If they want a relationship, dear, you allow them to do the reaching. You've plenty of time for that. I do pray that you will know my sister, Marigold, as I once did– witty and whimsical with the ability to lift spirits and lighten moods."

"I'd like that very much," I answered. "Shacklee does still pose a threat. He will not surrender to this equality easily. He continually attempts to veto all of Tavish's treaties. He's angered that the majority of the cabinet has yielded to Tavish's will. Shacklee makes me nervous, Ma. I long that he will withdraw, too, and take residence far away. A loose end, he is."

"Shacklee is a troubled man. He continues to idolize his father and the principles on which he was raised. But as you have learned, repentance and productive change is possible for everyone. Shacklee's heart may very well soften over time. He is in my prayers."

"And mine."

"You believe you'll stay there then? On the south side? Unlike Lolly?"

"I am very proud for Lolly, Ma. I saw her when I was over the bridge grocery shopping a few days ago. She looked right healthy...and independent. Aside from working at the boutique, she's now also waitressing at Paius. Says she's enjoying her lovely flat near Algirdis Square and hopes to have me over for supper once she's settled in. Her life is good, Ma, for the first time since I can remember."

"That gives me such peace." Ma heaved a collective sigh of relief.

"Pype and I do plan to stay here. So many still need our assistance. With the departure of those who opposed Tavish's rule and seceded, many trades have come available on the north side. Even here, printing work is offered at the *Sentry*, new farms and cattle need tending to and several of the derelict shops have reopened. There's talk of reopening the mill. But still, many of the elderly and sickly are without pay and food. They need our help. Mr. Gunnar continues to serve them while Pype is working on Rhoslynn Hill, but Pype and I feel led to stay right here. This has always been my home. I suppose it still is home, innit?"

"It is, dear Ursula," she answered. "And Mr. Huxley is still baking bread? Oden is coming along well?"

"Yeah. I've seen them both today."

"Two men," Ma said, "who would be destined to a life of misery, and an after-life of misery, if they had not been bathed in grace and mercy."

"Grace and mercy."

"And what of Finley? He's well and weaned from the Glabra tablets?"

"He's much better and devoting his time to his parents while his brother runs the pawn shop. We meet for tea on most Thursdays. Sometimes a northern girl he's recently met joins us. I think she's right good for him," I said. "Oh! Mr. Ames passed last week, Ma."

"He and Mora are finally reunited then."

"Are they there, Ma?"

"You know I cannot reveal the destiny of others, but I can say that they are reunited. I cannot disclose whether that is here or in fire."

"I pray they asked for the same mercy and grace that Oden and Barton did– that all of us must ask for daily."

"What of Stevenwill and Whitchurch's fate? Were they pardoned by the northern court last week?"

"No," I said. "They were found guilty of withholding information on Mora's whereabouts and sent to 2nd Street. Maybe I will visit them when I take Mr. Pethlen his supper one night. Maybe they should be versed on forgiveness?"

"That would be a good thing," Ma added. "I do enjoy hearing about all of these good things."

"Well, here's another then," I replied. "While doing data entry for the palladium mine this week, I noticed an increase in the accounting figures that I enter. I can only attribute it to Galvan and Chester working alongside one another during night shift. Production is up on their watch. They are good at what they do. Chester and Tulsee and all of their children are living in a fine home near the mine, but he and Galvan still find time for their meals at the diner," I said and sipped the tea.

"Are they there this evening?"

"No." I looked around the crowded restaurant. "Sunday night is quite the rush thanks to the popular sausage and speckled bread special. Galvan and Chester don't prefer the peak times. I think there is something sacred in their quiet meals of tenderloin and mashed sweet potatoes. Something revered about silently eating in the shadow of the old mill."

"I'm sure there is."

"Now that Bronwyn and Tabb can acquire many more things from the northern side, they've added new items to the menu. And Mr. Kestral contributes produce! His black thumb is a glowing shade of green now, Ma! He's traded his planter box for 75 square feet of lush soil at the edge of the woods. The rats in Dugald Alley sure hate the change."

Ma laughed. "This is all so lovely, Ursula, and so optimistic. Don't you see that you've done the ultimate good thing? Your kindness swayed one very important man. Your tender heart showed Tavish Dunbryll that you and your neighbors deserve to be treated with respect and equality. You and Pype opened his eyes to the beautiful truth regarding those who reside on the south side of the Winnow. You've represented the south well. You've represented love well. You've represented the Most High well. And when a man's ways please the Most High, he makes even his enemies to be at peace with him."

"Again, Ma, you give me too much—"

"That is why, Ursula, I will not be calling you anymore."

"What, Ma?" I asked, confused.

"My work is done, dear daughter."

"No."

"You've made amends with your father's killer, you've loved the unlovable, and you've managed to tear down walls of prejudice. Ursula, you've been receptive and allowed the Most High to do a wonderful work through you, and you will continue to be His vessel. You no longer need me to guide you."

"But I do, Ma!" I pleaded. "I always will!"

"Our sacred communication has been a beautiful and rare privilege, but it cannot go on forever."

My eyes began to water.

"You will continue doing good things, but don't you see, dear? Now it is time for you to receive good things…and you've found a wonderful thing in Pype Tyburn."

"Ma, I cannot bear to lose you. I can't bear to lose this. I can't let you go." I cried into the receiver. "Please don't leave me, Ma. Please. Not again. I still have so much to learn. I need you to teach me. I need you to guide me longer, Ma. I cannot let you go."

"You can let me go. You have the strength to do it. But, Ursula, I'll never completely be separated from you. The things I've taught you will remain. I will forever thrive in your heart and your memories. I'm on the spring wind that you crave and in the warmth of your coveted blackcurrant tea. I'm found in those things that bring you joy, Ursula. Forever I will be with you. Now. And eternity."

Heavy tears streamed from my dark eyes and dripped from the tip of my nose.

"You have grown into a wise and independent woman. You no longer require this. I have great faith that you will continue to succeed without a telephone call from me on Sunday evenings."

"I don't want to do this."

"But you can."

"I don't want this to end."

"But it must."

I sniffled. "May I ask one more favor though, Ma? I know it is not for you to disclose the destiny of another, but Papa? Please tell me, Ma. I beg. Please leave me with the comfort in knowing that you wait for me together."

"Ursula," Ma said, "you know that I cannot—"

"Please? I must know."

She paused. "Your father and I wait for you hand in hand."

I rested against the wall of the diner and tightly closed my eyes, but the tears managed to leak through and leave salty streaks on my face.

"Continue to good things, dear. I love you. Always."

"Please, Ma? Please don't—"

"Always, Ursula. Always."
I sobbed.
"Always."

I gently placed the damp receiver into the cradle and wiped my soaking face with the palms of my hands. When I turned, Bronwyn was sliding my supper plate onto the refurbished table.

"Everything quite alright?"

I sniffled and slid into the booth.

Bronwyn pointed to the seat across from me. "You mind?"

I shook my head before she sat down and folded her chubby hands on the table top.

"Ursula, I see your sorrow and tears. Have the conversations with your sweet mother come to an end?"

"You-"

"Yes, I suspected that's who you were speaking to all this time," she said. "I've never personally known anyone favored enough to receive regular crossover calls and personal guidance from the other side. That's a right blessing."

"But I don't know how to carry on now, Bronwyn. I don't know how to let her go. I still need my mother."

"Dear," Bronwyn said, "there comes a time when we must forget what lies behind and press forward to what lies ahead. Yes, this sacred time with your mother has come to an end, but the Most High is doing a new thing. A new beginning– *now it springs forth.*"

I silently nodded.

"Wipe your tears, dear girl." She reached across the table and grabbed my hand. "For you are favored. You are blessed. You are fortunate, Ursula Underwood. You are fortunate, indeed."

Fortunate, indeed.

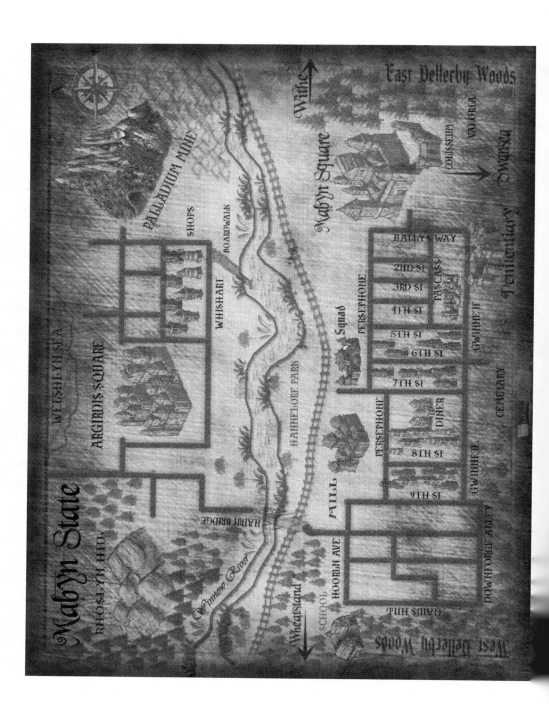

A WORD FROM THE AUTHOR

So, this was different, right?

What's a Runyon tree? And Macron juice? What year did this take place? Cobblestone streets? A mystical payphone? Who in the world says "innit" instead of "isn't it"?

The imagination is a glorious thing, *innit*?

Barton Huxley popped into my head on an Alabama highway while my husband drove us home from Florida in October 2016. Barton Huxley did not have a name, but I could clearly see him— a homeless man in a dingy polyester suit resting on a corner with a mug and cardboard sign. He was so vivid, so clear, and I could hardly wait to bring him to life on paper. I was eager to invent people around him— people who passed him on that street corner every day. I was so eager that I wrote the first paragraph of this book in the passenger seat of my car on that Alabama highway.

I knew I wanted to write a different novel. I wanted to put the wit of *Suspicion on Sugar Creek* and the Lifetime Movie Network-esque drama of *Ten Years Taken* aside and make up an entirely new world. I drew the dystopian streets of this pretend city on notebook paper (which my friend Chad so brilliantly brought to life on the previous page. Thank you!) I imagined each apartment, derelict building and the piles of charred brick on Bally's Way. It was the perfect setting for the homeless man born in my head.

This book was fun to write, too. I believe one of the biggest joys I found while working on it was inventing names for the characters. While doing some inspirational Googling, I landed on a page of Welsh names and stayed there for quite a long time. So maybe this takes place somewhere near Wales? Even I don't know. It's possible. But with the imagination, all things are.

When I started this story, I did not intend on incorporating such a religious theme. It kind of happened along the way. I think the Lord was nudging me to tell the story of His loving mercy. We are all undeserving of it, but He so graciously and freely offers it if we just ask. Nothing we can do can separate us from His love.

I have many to thank for helping me bring that homeless man and his neighbors to life.

To my husband and children— thanks for understanding my need to write all night, therefore prohibiting me from being a cordial morning person who cooks hot breakfasts.

To my sister, Carmen— thank you for being my biggest fan. I love you more than you know.

To my creative cohort, Anna Lind Thomas— thanks for your support and your Photoshop magic. I hope you will read this book quicker than you read my other two. I'm kidding. Kind of.

To my talented friend, Jill Bell— thank you for painting the cover and bringing life to the picture in my head. You are so insanely talented, and I thank the Good Lord for your friendship.

To my editor, Beth Nolan— thank you for loving this book as much as I do and helping me control, my, passion, for, commas.

To my community and all of my friends, fans and followers— thank you for the beautiful support and encouragement.

To my beautiful mother, Susan Ann, in Heaven— call me. I could still use your guidance. I love you. Always.

Made in the USA
San Bernardino, CA
21 June 2017